MW01242596

Some of the characters are based on the people in my life,
those that I wish to honour for their great influence.
Otherwise all else is fictional and any situations or likenesses
are purely coincidental.

ISBN: 978-1499708530
ISBN-13: 149970853X

*This book is dedicated in loving memory of*
*Ashley LaTara Reese Sparks, who could read whole books in*
*a day, and loved to read more than I love to write. Her*
*kindness and sheer joy for life was out of this world. Maybe*
*that's why she had to leave.*

# CHAPTER 1

I can hardly believe I made it up those 14 flights of stairs. I'm tired, I'm pissed. I pay $1500 a month on this snazzy downtown Austin apartment and they can't fix the only elevator? Along the way, I stop to vomit just a little- I'm hungover. I wish I could say this is a rare occasion, but it isn't. The only thing that's different in this equation is that I'm coming home to my place and not another hotel room.

I stumble toward my door and fumble with a heavy set of jingling keys like Santa on his merry sleigh but with far less glee- none in fact- until I manage to make a perfect match, pushing the door open in great haste for another journey to the restroom. I hug the toilet like we're best friends long awaiting each other's gracious presence. I am, it's not.

I think about the building's main doors. They are quite pristine with a frosted glass tint, which I'm sure makes people confused when they see a goon like me strutting on in like I belong somewhere that screams posh. The doors say "A A" which stands for Austin Apartments. I always had a good laugh in the past when I thought of it as walking into an AA meeting. But now that it feels I actually need to attend AA, seems like the cruelest joke in the world. Old me is laughing from above, maybe even paying some pigeon to take a dump on my head as I enter.

After a sweet release of whatever was left in me, 4 stouts and maybe even a kidney too, I hop up and brush my teeth. I know I won't be kissing or breathing near anyone but it's the proper thing to do. I could at least try to wow me! It's nearing 2pm and I've just flown home from a "business trip." I went on a 6 month excursion across the United States and a few Canadian locations (my home country) opening for Tim Tanning in my new adventure to becoming a glorified stand up comedian. It was a dream come true to hear people laughing at my self deprecating jokes night after night, even if immediately afterwards I fell back into the reality that I tried to leave behind in Austin.

*What are you doing here?*

I thought I had seen a box on my sprint to the crapper and sure enough, I was right. There's a box sitting there. It was supposed to be gone by now. Livid, I walk up to it and take a peek inside. The contents are all his. Or should I say, ours. That cock sucker. I gave him six fucking months to get his shit out of my apartment and he leaves this behind. Was this his way of telling me to suck it?

I don't want to be reminded of the one thing I tried hard to forget so I throw it to the floor as if making a loud noise will echo over and let him know I hate him, even more than before.

I flop onto my cushy ash gray sofa like the dead fish that I am and reach into my very empty purse for some cheap aspirin. Unlike most successful women with a purse full of make up, fun sized toiletries, and a lot of other unnecessary junk, I keep it pretty simple: a zip lock bag of medicines, one condom, car keys, chap stick, and a notepad. I travel light and don't really do the make up thing. Maybe it's because make up and I are a total lost cause. There isn't enough make up in the world to hide the screaming layers of my shiny bowling ball like forehead, the tired tea bags below my eyes, or the deep wrinkles of my sarcasm that have made me a genuine stand up comedian.

When the pill has enjoyed its *Schlitterbahn* water park ride down my alcohol infused throat, I lay my head back and attempt to rub my temples. I hear a lot of noise from outside: foot stomping and movement. I assume there is a big Texas dance affair going on in the hall and mind my own business again.

I still can't believe he left that box here. I guess he really did want to leave all of me behind.

I manage to fall asleep for an hour or two, having grown accustomed to the noise going on in the hallway. Here I lay again, still not sure of what I should do today. Clearly, I'm free. I've worked my bony ass off for the last 6 months and now I'm on a vacation the way every comedian hopes to have. Except I'm not happy for this void in my life. I wasn't ready to come home. Part of me secretly enjoyed hotel rooms, bus rides with Tim, and eating out every night. Too bad nobody ate me out.

I make myself a cup of coffee and enjoy the dark roast smells that go whirling around my head like those damn tasty smelling bread ovens when you pass a *Subway*. I never think I want to pay someone what I can easily do at home until I smell that bread and then I'm all, damnit! I'm gonna go spend $7 because I smelled some fucking good bread. I'm hungry I quickly decide when I feel a pang of emptiness in my tummy calling out to me, probably from thinking about bread. I like to think of my stomach as a baby I'm having. It's very demanding and when it needs something, it has no shame in calling out to me no matter what situation I may be in. The baby vomits, the baby gets hungry. The baby has to take a really bad crap and doesn't care that no restroom is around for miles. My baby also doesn't seem to mind having to take dumps on airplanes. That was a first.

I open my sleek aluminum fridge and am immediately reminded that I haven't been home in half a year. AKA my fridge is emptier than *Al Bundy's*. There is one thing though, something I completely forgot about. I had tried to cook myself a little breakfast before I left as a way to prove that I could be totally independent in this newly solo household. So here sits a 7 month old stack of pancakes that looks worse than my face. I overlook the mold on the side and cannot help but truly see myself in those flapjacks. That's what I was to my husband: mold. I grew on him into such a disgusting substance that he was both mentally and physically sick of me. If I really did look as bad as that green fungi, I guess I would have left me too.

I decide I'll go visit my favourite place instead (that's right, I don't even bother to throw it out), a hipsterish Japanese fast food joint on Guadalupe called *Zen*. Okay, okay, this is Austin; every place is meant to attract hipsters. And because I'm a classless douche, I don't change my clothes from the garb I sported on my flight from LAX to Austin Bergstrom International. I know it stinks of my sweat, but who the fuck is gonna smell me?

As I'm locking the door from the inside while stepping into the hall, I notice someone entering next door. That apartment had been vacant for almost a year now.

This man along side me looks so familiar, I quickly recognize. He's rather tall, definitely attractive and working the charm of his very gingerly hair. And that's when it strikes me. I know this guy. And I don't know him personally, I know him the way any woman can turn into a fan girl at the drop of a celebrity's name. Holy hell. It couldn't be...

"Hi, I just moved in," this sexy motherfucker smiles and extends his hand. He doesn't seem to mind that I'm staring at him like he just told me that he was Jesus or some other holy figure you may or may not worship.

This is where I have a sort of transformation if you will. I turn into a forest green, slimy frog and my limbs all turn to putty. My body extends in only a way that a cartoon character can. My hands hit the ground in their lifeless shock. My mouth falls open too, extending a few feet down. My eyes have turned into large eggs that cannot take their viewership away from Cory fucking Koenig. That's pronounced KAY-NIG, which is a joke in and of itself. To avoid saying a word seen as offense, I won't explain this. We will call this frog version of me, oh I don't know, Reginald? Reginald the Frog is it.

"Are you Cory Koenig?!" I blurt out. The look he gives me in retort is priceless. I think maybe he thinks I just told him I was Jesus or whoever! But I don't care, I'm too busy studying the gorgeous light blue eyes and perfect teeth he's presenting me with.

"Yeah, I am. I can't tell you how surprised I am that you know that," he laughs with the most adorable grin as he pushes open his new door.

"Holy shit! No way this is happening! I'm from Ottawa and I am a HUGE Partisans fan, so to think that a former Partisan is living next door is just, wow! Seriously, I would have a better shot of winning the lottery, eh?"

"I guess you'd better go buy a ticket," he tilts his head to look at me better. He's practically a foot taller than me, meaning all the more sexy body of his to gawk at.

"I promise I'm not always this squirmy. And I'm so, so, sorry you got traded in the off season dude. Assassins suck!"

"Tell me about it! I really thought I'd spend my entire career in Ottawa. How did I go from a legendary Canada team to a sunbelt team that hasn't made the playoffs since I got drafted? The only good that will come of this is that almost no one will know who I am here. Do you think I'll get recognized?"

"Honestly? No. No one recognizes me either."

Cory looks befuddled about this statement; his lip hangs as he argues with himself for what to say. He quickly avoids eye contact in fear I will see how hard he is skimming for any kind of recognition. Clearly, he doesn't know who I am. Also, I said 'how hard he is'... that's what she said!

"Oh, are you, uh, someone?" he squints, his cheeks slightly blushing. He probably feels bad for my poor wounded ego. The only thing he has wounded is my underwear. Now they're all wet and need to be cleaned again after I just got the poop stain off.

"I'm a stand up comedian," I admit rather shyly. I was somebody until an actual somebody showed up next door.

"Wow cool! What's your name?"

"Jiles Perry."

"I'm sorry to say I'm not familiar with your work," he chews on his bottom lip, giving me a quick look over to see if anything about me may be familiar.

"It's okay, I'm new. I just got back from a tour and shortly I'll be filming my first hour special. I'm pretty stoked!" I gush, even if I know he doesn't give a shit.

"That's awesome, I'll definitely check it out."

"Do you know who Tim Tanning is?"

"I love Tim! I saw him last month in Ottawa!"

"Really? I opened that show."

"Yeah, about that," Cory snickers with a lopsided grin. "I tend to show up after opening acts. I only want to see who I paid for ya know? Sorry."

"Don't be, opening acts normally suck! Can't say I haven't missed the national anthem at a game."

"So uh, I'm going to start unpacking now."

This is clearly a lie to end the small talk. Who the fuck wants to unpack? I don't mind this since my stomach baby is about to start throwing a giant hissy fit in front of someone I want to eat for dinner.

"I would love to help you but I don't want to. I'm hungry, care to join me?"

"Actually I just ate and I need to get started. I've got a meeting early tomorrow with my new staff anyway."

"Okay, well, if you need any information or just someone to bitch to about how badly the Assassins suck, I'm always here."

"Duly noted, thanks Jules."

"Jiles."

"Right, sorry Jiles. See you around."

He enters his new home and I start skipping to the elevator as if I was feeling this good all day. I cannot believe it. How did that hunky bastard wind up next door to my shabby self? He's dreamy, an absolute piece of ass I'd give anything to bone. I quickly think about how I'll be able to hear him having sex and see his one night stands leave. That's how I roll. I always think of the worst things that could happen because, when don't they?

I stop skipping as soon as I realize I have to walk down 14 flights of stairs. It would be less painful for me to jump off my balcony.

# CHAPTER 2

I come home still terribly caught up in the euphoria that Cory Koenig is my new neighbor. I also bitch about the stairs the entire time too.

Over my stag dinner I wondered if Cory will give me the hook up for tickets. I also wondered if I will hook up with him. I doubt he'd have any real interest in me. The guy's got money and he's an athlete. He's probably got puck bunnies lined up around the block of our building waiting for a chance to see his dong. Then again, this is Austin. I bet he could walk passed 300 people and maybe one person could say they recognize his face but don't know exactly where from. But this still doesn't mean I have a chance with him. After all, he's him and I'm me.

As soon as I enter my apartment I start wondering what he's doing at this very instant. Call it juvenile and only done on TV shows, but I decide there is something I must try.

I go into my kitchen and rummage through my cool beer glasses I've gotten from various brewery tours and whatnot, opting for the longest one. I got this one in a stout drinking competition. I smoked quite a few people chugging that shit.

Back inside my bedroom, I press the glass against the wall I share with Cory's bedroom and push my ear to the end. What do you know? This shit actually works! But he's not talking. I just hear the slight racket from whatever show he is watching. The fact that we share bedroom walls bothers me slightly. I know this because I toured his apartment before I selected mine. I've only lived here for a year since I "made it" only recently and thus far have had the luxury of basically having this entire floor to myself. I wonder if I'll hear his orgasms through these walls. He sure as hell won't be hearing any from me. Maybe to trick him into thinking I have a life, I could play someone's homemade porn loud enough and make him think it's me. I'll just memorize one until I can remember to mute it when some other girl's name is called. Then I'll mute it and insert my name above while I'm jumping on the bed.

That'll do.

It's only 9pm on a Friday but I have no life so I reach into my closet for my favourite pajamas that I didn't take on tour because I couldn't make an ass of myself in front of the connections I would make. You probably assume I have a sexy piece of lingerie or maybe just some booty shorts but nope. These are my favourite: my red adult footy pajamas with a moose pattern. I love moose for no normal reasoning whatsoever. It started when I saw this moose doll in an Edmonton jersey at a truck stop in Saskatoon, Saskatchewan. Goofy name, I know. If you think that's funny you should know there's a city there called Regina. It's pronounced *Reh-geyena*. Yup. The city that rhymes with fun, my pal Lynette says.

I thought the moose was so cute but at the time I was broke and he was a whopping $20 CAD. I also felt I was too old to buy a stuffed moose. So I took his picture to remember his cute face and went along my way. Like a sick need for some women to buy a "must have" designer shoe, scarf or bubble gum (I don't know!), I suddenly thought about that damn moose every day. I told myself next time I came back I would buy him but it was almost a year later when I finally passed through again. My heart pounded in ridiculous excitement as I sped into the *Flying J* parking lot, waiting to be reunited with my moose that I had named Albert Louis Moose. It's pronounced *Albeh Louhwee*. He's French Canadian.

So when I got to the store and ran around looking frantically for my long lost moose, I only found these lame looking dog and cat dolls with marbles for peepers. I sulked my way over to the *Denny's*, ordered a hot stack of pancakes, and cried like a baby over my meal. I was so disappointed, I felt like I had lost my child. My husband only told me to get over myself, it was just a stuffed animal. But I never saw him as just a doll.

A week later I was on my way to Montreal and I stopped at the same store in London, Ontario. I took a peek and sure enough, they had their own slew of cute moose dolls in Toronto and Montreal jerseys. While my Pierre Moose (I chose Montreal to honour Albert's French heritage) is totally adorable and my travel buddy on my comedy tour, he's sadly never been able to fill the void of poor Albert Louis Moose, the one that got away.

So over the years of my amateur comedian travels, I managed to get a whole family of them. There's Pierre of course and his brothers Jacques, Jacques Jr., Remy, Claude, Maxime, Andre, Elliot, Plastic Figurine, Francois, Christmas Decoration, Sleepy Time, and Maurice Moose. And one day, I'll find that Albert if it's the last thing I do. Since the collection of my moose family, I've picked up other moose-ish items along the way. Like these lame adult pajamas. But whatever, I'm not fucking anyone so I'll wear what I want to bed.

I get in my moose jammies and fix myself a cup of hot

chocolate like it every actually gets cold in Austin. I climb
into bed with the moose family and look at their innocent
little faces, the only joy I will surely have in my life for
some time.

"I love you little guys," I say and give them all a kiss on
their fluffy, brown snouts. I'd better get used to kissing furry
shit, that's all I'm gonna get for a while. Unless I suck a fat
dude's dick who doesn't shave.

I decide I'll watch some of the home movies that were
taken of my act along the tour so I can see where I fucked up
and what worked, what didn't. I don't think I'd ever need to
re-watch my wedding video to try to fix those mistakes. I
would never be able to pinpoint what went wrong.

# CHAPTER 3

I suppose the courteous thing to do would be to tell you about my husband. Or ex rather. His name is, drum roll please...

"Ford Richardson! Come on down! You're the next contestant on "Fuck Up Jiles Perry's Life!"

Yes, he does sound like a fucking car dealership. I met him in college at *UTA*, that's the *University of Texas at Austin* for those of you who are unfamiliar. He was the studious type, the shy guy, never went out to party. I was the same way. I know that's odd behaviour for the ground work of a comedian but hey, we can't all be heroin shooters fighting to suppress memories of having a dick up our buttholes, using comedy as a means to tackle the situations head on.

It was love at first sight. We both looked up from our milk cartons and eyed each other behind our thickly rimmed Buddy Holly glasses in the pre hipster era. When we both saw that we were wearing a button up shirt with a pocket holding pens colour organized, we knew we were meant to be. And because I didn't know I was lactose intolerant, I ran off to take a wicked shit before I introduced myself.

Ford and I would get together for study dates in the library, getting a table in the back to work on math and any other topics that were taken by brute force that had nothing to do with our degrees. He majored in finance and works as an investment banker downtown. Me? I majored in creative writing and I'm making way more than him, hizzah! Because he and I both hated football and completely ignored the existence of the *Longhorns*, we could find nights to be completely alone in the library, dorm, and other campus hangouts. It was one of those nights when I lost my virginity in my dorm room. I thought that meant he and I would be together forever, because I was one of those goons that thought if I waited until I met someone I loved, it would last as long as a *Disney* fairy tale. We were just like *Aladdin;* I was his magic carpet ride.

He proposed to me about a year after we achieved some monetary success post grad and got an apartment in Pfluggerville together. Fun fact: the middle school football field was the set of the popular football drama, *Friday Night Lights*. Of course, I don't give a shit because I hate football.

He proposed to me on stage at *Cap City Comedy Club* during an open mic night. He said he had a set to do after me and I fell for it. I guess I should have known since he barely had any funny bones in his body. After my act the announcer asked me to stay on stage and then he walked on. I was so confused until he got down on his knees. At the time I thought it was the most precious thing anyone had ever done for me. And like any 22 year old idiot who thinks they have met the one oh so young, I said yes. We were hitched a few months later at a backyard ceremony in his parent's very well to do West Lake abode. There were never any inclinations that we weren't going to work out. We never fought, we certainly had no financial issues. We went together like gin and tonic, *Snooki* and tans, rappers and big booty hoes.

I had won Austin's local comedy competition, *"Who is the Funniest Person in Austin?,"* and with that new exposure I was granted a lot of bookings around the state and beyond.

I guess he may have gotten tired of waiting for me, or maybe just tired of me. Perhaps the fact that we never fought meant neither of us had any passion. We kind of just settled into ourselves and took what we thought was easy into the next step. They say relationships are work. For us, that work felt like we were on welfare. We did nothing, kept riding the coattails of life, and blew all our money on rims for our cars. Kidding! I hate that shit.

So here's the big bummer you've been waiting for.

He left me for someone else. It hit me like that giant frozen ham that got thrown at Paula Deen's head. It was all one day we were fine, the next day, he's chunking a deuce at me. He didn't tell me how they met or who she was, but I quickly found out when I saw them together. That was the last time I saw him. During his big break up speech he said I could have the apartment. I guess it was his idea of a consolation prize.

The very next month I was on my comedy tour with a bag of jokes in one hand, a broken heart in the other. I lived life recklessly for that entire tour, living completely up to the persona of a comedian: a drunk party animal. I did a few drugs here and there, and drank more than I ever drank in college. Tim had asked me if I was okay because he knew beforehand that I wasn't a user so I told him the story. He made me laugh and told me I'd feel a lot better when I had my own TV show and DVD and he'd be stuck in Austin working in an office where he couldn't fart because everyone would hear it.

Over the months I felt better but I always knew that when I would get home, seeing the place without his knickknacks would hurt. It bothered me just a little. Not so much that his stuff was gone, but because he left behind our mementos as if he never wanted to think of me again.

I know that time will heal all and that I have a lot of great things going for me, but there isn't a distraction big enough on this planet that will let me forget about this whole *Maury Show* routine any time soon. Except maybe the fact that there is a penis a few feet away from my head that I'd really like to have at.

# CHAPTER 4

I am awoken by a terribly early call. 6am in fact.

"Who is it?" I mumble.

"Hey it's Ben. Sorry to wake you. How sober are you?"

"You'll be proud to know I had not a drop to drink last night."

He doesn't need to know that drinks before 5pm do not constitute as "last night."

"Excellent. Can you come to the studio and fill in for Brodie this entire week?"

A pause. He knows this will take much explaining to do. I'm talking payment, death, etc.

"She got really sick last night and needed to go to the hospital. They asked her to take the week off and I couldn't find any other subs last minute."

"Oh yeah? I could use something to live for. I'll be there as soon as I can."

Even if I am totally not ecstatic to wake up at this god forsaken hour, I am pleased to know I'll have a daily activity for a week. More time I won't spend thinking about Ford. I decide I'll live up to my comedy standards and walk out of my apartment in my moose jammies.

Within 10 minutes I am pulling into 94X, the alternative rock station's parking lot. You would think it's this totally suave building in a great area with amenities galore, but nope. Situated along the service road of I-35 in a less than welcoming area, the building is old and the parking lot sucks.

"Jiles Perry, requested by sir Ben White," I tell the receptionist when she gives me the once over as if my pajamas are worse than her old lady get up. Whoever said floral and stripes were cool may have been crazier than me.

They send me in during a commercial break where I find Ben White waiting for me with a pair of chunky headphones in his hands. He's your traditional lazy guy: overweight and always in a nasty ass old hat. But, he's so goddamn funny that I've always found him attractive. Not to mention he happens to have my favorite trait: red hair.

Along side him are two producers, Dustin and Mark. Dustin is a nerd, Mark is a druggie, and Ben is the every man. Brodie is the female voice of reason with a sexy Australian accent; how she got here I'll never know. It's a great mix of different minded folk coming together to make you piss your pants on the way to work or during your morning masturbation if you're into that shit. I listen a lot and came on the show a few times after I got some notoriety.

"You made it! Thank God, no way I could do this show without a vagina in the room," Ben snickers as he pats the seat aside him.

"This vagina is covered up like hell right now so I doubt you'll find it. I didn't shave my entire tour. Why bother?" I admit, plopping down on this high end black recliner seat, sitting Indian style as I place my set on.

"What the hell are you wearing?"

"Hey Benny, you called me at 6 in the morning and told me to hustle like *Superman*. I spent half of that time looking for a phone booth to change. Did you know telephone booths don't exist anymore? I think now they're hobo urinals."

"Alright, I'll give you that. We're about to do the sports segment so I'll introduce you in the next slot. We will be talking about our weekends."

The 'On Air' light comes up and the little audio snippet of the station plays before Ben takes over. I ignore the football banter and lucky for me, because no one cares about hockey in Texas, he fails to mention those ASS-assins and how they're about to play their first game of the season. I doze off a little until Mark throws a baby stapler at my boob. My body shoots up immediately and I toss it at him while he laughs for getting me in the breast. He has terribly good aim because I have very little breast to target. If I were Dolly Parton, even an autistic kid could get that shot. It might even bounce back too, all of that fake rubber or whatever is in a fake boob.

"We're back on, I'll introduce you now," Ben prepares.

"We've got a special guest in studio for the rest of the week, local comedian on the rise Mrs. Jiles Perry. Thanks for coming in Jiles."

"Screw you man, you woke me up during a hot dream and asked me to come work for free. Do you even know how much bad karma you have coming your way?"

"I know, I know. The dream was about me. You can just come over to my place afterward and I'll make sure the dream is completed."

"If I come over you can finish the dream but I'll probably be asleep during the whole thing."

"Well good morning to you too. Jiles is filling in for Brodie this week, as I mentioned earlier she's sick and the doctor recommended she stay at home for the entire week. Part of that sounds like a lie but hey, I'd make it up too for a week off. Jiles, what'd you do this weekend?

"What did I do, what did I do? I got back from my first stand up comedy tour."

"That's right, Jiles opened for Tim Tanning on a huge tour across all of the US and Canada. Jiles was the last winner of the *"Funniest Person in Austin"* competition, but I guess she lost her crown since she is only wearing moose footy pajamas today."

"They didn't give me a crown, they gave me a golden cane and I broke it beating up the last guy who made fun of my comfortable pajamas."

"How do you piss with that get up in the middle of the night?"

"There's a trap door on the back."

"Does this mean you're ready to go if I want to get it on?"

"I would debate you, but the answer is yes."

Ben goes to hit a button for a sound affect but nothing plays. We sit silently for three seconds. He glares at the computer for a minute before turning to me. "Nothing works around here. Not even us."

**W**hen the show is over, we go over topics for tomorrow and Ben asks if I have anything I'd like to promote. I mention that I'll be doing a live taping shortly and that I have a good number of tickets we could give away for prizes. Otherwise I tell him the show is his and I'm just a guest. When Dustin and Mark have left, he asks me something a bit more personal that we'd never discuss on air.

"What happened to your wedding ring?"

"Pawned it for drug money but the *Pawn Stars* said it was worthless."

"Jiles," he peers downward, giving me this downward glance like an angry parent knowing their kid just lied about pissing the bed. 'I know it was you. Dad's too old to piss the bed. Actually...'

"Ford left me," I say matter of fact-ly.

"Are you telling me that dealership left you?"

"I sure am."

Ben takes this harder than I thought he would. He and I also met in college during a few classes on his journey to a Radio, TV, and Film degree. He was one of the football loving guys (too lazy to play himself) but afterwards he'd pig out with me in the cafeteria and we'd swap jokes. He always believed in my comedy career and supported me during stand up shows when no one was in the audience. He's a good dude who also has been divorced. We're a bunch of fools, getting married young.

"We should start a First Husband's Club. After all, I was the man in that marriage. I made more money than little rich boy of West Lake."

"When did this happen?" Ben inquires.

"About 7 months ago. It was right before my tour. I'm sorry I didn't tell you. I just kind of stayed drunk on the entire tour so I didn't do much talking to anyone. I didn't do much explaining beyond telling my family that my marriage was over."

"Damn, I'm so sorry Jiles. What a douche bag. I never liked *Subaru*."

"Ford."

"*Nissan?*" he tries. I laugh and shake my head.

"Thank you for the wake up call. I really needed another distraction. Maybe even something to live for."

"You're always welcome here kid. Let's hang out this weekend. I'll get you back into the swing of life in no time. You can be my first student in the Ben White Divorce Program."

"Sign me up," I pick up a pen and wave my hand with a fake air signature of my name. We both stare at each other with simple smirks, reasoning to me that this is the first and most intimate connection either of us have had in a while.

# CHAPTER 5

I get home around 10:30am thanks to light traffic. It's probably a nice schedule to have in the grand scheme of things, but I don't think I could ever get used to waking up at 5:00am every weekday, even if I got home just 5 hours later. In fact, the first thing I do when I get home is jump back into my bed and promptly fall asleep.

I wake up on my own doings at 2pm, which is probably the time I would have waken up regardless of being on the Ben and Brodie show. I remind myself I'll need to go to sleep a tad earlier today so I can get into the swing of things. I toss a *K Cup* into the machine to shake those still lingering morning symptoms. I've never been able to get rid of the bags from below my eyes. People must think I get no sleep, but the truth is I'm just ugly. In lieu of feeling ugly, I decide I'll jump on my scale and see what kind of damage I've done on this tour of the nations finest junk food. *Bojangles, White Castle, In and Out, Rallys*: you name it, I had it. I close my eyes for a minute as I take deep breaths, looking down to see these flashing numbers: 101.

How the fuck did I do that? I pat myself on the back, supposing fast food agrees with me. I look up at the mirror and take a good look at my face. This is the face that *Hyundai* got tired of looking at. He got sick of these small, unbowed lips. He got tired of my simple nose, my hardly arched eyebrows. The brown of my eyes no longer called out to him like truffles. My slightly pudgy cheeks must have been too child like. That's probably why he left that box behind. He didn't want to see this anymore. I wish I didn't either. I imagine that I walk away in the mirror version of myself and see what it looks like to be invisible.

"Hey good looking, you look like you don't cost a dime to take to dinner, how about we go to the finest joint in town, my treat?" I wink at my ghost. I can't help it. I have to make a joke about everything. That's how I protect my emotions, by finding a reason to laugh.

The hours of the day are spent with me haphazardly finding things to do that I feel might or might not be of importance. Like: clipping my toe nails, taking out the trash, tweezing my muppet eye brows, washing the dishes I didn't do before the tour, trimming the pubes just a tad, and watering the plants that died over the tour. Oh, and I stopped for my hour dose of the *Maury Show*. It's the only way I can feel better about myself, watching people who are clearly more depressed than I am. I mean, poor Maury! Having to deal with all of those trashy people on a daily basis.

"You can do it Nicky!" I say to the poinsettia plant that has long since wilted, hoping my words of encouragement will bring it back to life. Through the glass I hear a knock on my door. Did I order a pizza in the mix of my housekeeping/woman-scaping? Sounds like something I would do.

I find him in all of his glory standing there. Not *Chevy*, it's freaking Cory Koenig.

"Hu-Hey," I say, thinking quickly about how I'm in a pair of boxers and old Partisans tee. I quickly feel Reginald the frog attempting to transform my body but I keep my composure together.

"Is this a bad time?"

"No no, I was just trying to bring my plants back to life. Come in," I usher him in, closing the door behind as I take a peek at his ass. Damn. Those blue jeans are shaping his figure for my pleasure.

"I figured I'd do the neighborly thing and ask if you wanted to join me for dinner. It's my first 'night on the town' and I have no idea where to go, I just know I don't want to end up on 6th street or somewhere cliche."

"No I got ya, you don't want to find yourself there unless you want to wake up beside an under-ager with a fake ID."

That's probably not true, but anything that keeps him to myself helps! He's looking at me waiting for a yes or a no, a coy smile hangs in the balance of my response.

"Yeah, sure, let me just get dressed right quick."

"Oh, well I can give you some time. I know how you women are."

"You don't know me at all then. Feel free to enjoy your apartment backwards," I call out from my bedroom.

"Why are you in boxers?"

"Because the penis opening slot is so convenient when I want to scratch my crotch."

"I love your honesty," he laughs from the living room.

I quickly toss on a pair of jeans myself, some that will never make me look as good as he does. I decide to leave the hockey tee behind so as to not draw attention to him. That means I only have a few choices left, so I grab a buffalo check button up and toss it over a wife beater.

"Ready?" I ask, going after my featherlight purse on the sofa.

"Wow you are the fastest woman ever. Are you *Superman* or something?"

I think to myself what I said to Ben this morning about changing like *Superman* and smile warmly within; maybe we will have more in common than I think.

**W**e step out of the building and start our journey on Cesar Chavez Boulevard, walking east alongside the gorgeous view of Lady Bird Lake as I try to quickly think of a place Cory might enjoy. After all, his first meal at the hands of my decision will be a big part of his overall thoughts on me. I can't take him to *Pluckers* or *Bikinis*, I want him to think I'm classy. If I weren't trying to impress him, we'd be at *Whataburger*.

"There is a joint a few blocks down called *Trio*, they have a bit of everything. A bit upscale, but decent prices."

"Sure, we don't need to go far."

We're there within 5 minutes, quickly finding a model type hostess with an obviously fake grin hoping for tips or to meet a rich guy who ask if he can order her for dessert. I stare at her highlights and think about how I always associate highlights with the trash I see on the *Maury Show*. I've mentioned *Maury* three times now, can you tell I'm a fan?

She looks at Cory with a gaze of wonder, probably wondering what he's doing with me. She seats us at a two top in the centre of the room, setting down his menu first. I take offense to her obvious disdain for my existence but I quickly forgive her when I realize she probably thinks I'm a guy with long hair.

"Your server will be with you in just a moment," she flashes him her *Chick-let* sized teeth and sways in her walk, hoping he's looking.

"I'm sorry about that," he comments.

"What?"

"I didn't like her body language, she clearly thinks she's going to get me or something. I hate when I go to a restaurant and the female employees try to make the women feel like shit. Do they really think they'll get a bigger tip when they flirt in front of mixed company?"

I'm taken by his words, impressed that he wants to defend me when he has no reason to do so. I blush slightly, grabbing hold of my menu to take a peak.

"It's okay, I know people can't figure out why I'm with you."

"Well she must not know that you're the famous Jiles Perry, the ginger lover extraordinaire."

I drop my menu like it's covered in hot butter, a stark realization that he may know more about me than he initially lead on.

"How d-do you know that?" I stutter. Stuuu...tuu..stutt..er.

"I googled you."

"You googled moi?" I point to myself, a little too much emphasis on 'moi.'

"Yeah, why not? Don't tell me you didn't google me," the sultry athlete leans back in his chair, letting me admire just how tall he is. Gosh, his face, that leg, those abs. I cannot see them but I know what's there. He is just so...is he on the menu? I'll take a buffet of that, please. Stop drooling, speak Jiles, speak!

"I didn't have to, I already know. I'm a fan, remember?"

"Damn that's right. I thought it would be cool to know who was living next door. I checked everything just in case you were a convicted felon or a sex offender. Turns out you're just a sex offender to get away from children."

"You listened to my act?"

"Yeah, I found some videos on *YouTube*."

"I'm so flattered. That's really cool of you, Cory."

"It was hilarious, you're really good. Let me know when your living taping is, I'd love to come."

"In me," I mutter.

"Huh?"

"Nothing. So, we drinking?" I ask before it seeps into my memory that I have to be in bed early.

"Nah, I have an early morning skate. Tomorrow is my first game!"

"Oh yeah, cool. Who are ya'll playing?"

"Carolina, not really the hardest. You should come!"

"Uh, the thing is, I kind of hate the Assassins. I mean, I really hate them."

"Really?" Cory burrows his eyebrows, watching for whatever lame explanation I might have. He cocks his head to the side and I try to resist whatever it is in his sexy blue eyes that make me almost want to attend.

"I only go when my Partisans come through town."

"How did you wind up here of all places?"

"I wanted to start a new life and I wanted somewhere with the exact opposite feel of Ottawa. So I went from cold as balls to sweaty balls."

"Do you have any family here?" he asked.

"Not really, just a few cousins but I pretty much keep to myself."

Koenig gives me a look of pure sympathy. A look he'd give to the opposing team while shaking their hands post beating them off the playoff route. Hehe, beating them off.

"Hey, I'm not a Sara McLaughlin charity dog! I'm

loaded, I can afford to live where you live!"

"You seeing anyone?"

As I quickly contemplate how I will explain that I just got thrown back on the pile of stinky fish at the meat market minus sounding pathetic, a male server comes over to our table.

"Good evening, I'm Russ and I'll be your server this evening. Can I get you started with some drinks? We have a fabulous champagne on special tonight, one of the finest brands imported into Texas," he announces like a *Price is Right* product. I can tell he's gay immediately. I can't decide if this is good or bad. Will he treat me like the hostess?

"Actually no boozing for us tonight," Cory says. "I'll take a *Coke*. Jiles?"

"Diet."

"Alright, I'll give you both a minute with the menus," he softly adds, walking away with just as much shake to his booty as the hostess.

"Maybe it's a requirement to shake your ass when you walk here," Cory mentions, having looked back to see for himself.

"Nah, I think he just wants you too."

"You got gaydar?"

"World's finest. Don't worry. I'm not a lesbian. There's gotta be a few funny ladies that love the cock."

"So, where were we? Oh, I asked if you were seeing anyone," Cory reiterates, making me gulp once again. I see the server in the corner of my eye coming back with two glasses. I decide I'll make funny noises until he has returned.

"I, uh, golly geez, hmmm, ohhhh, hey our drinks are here!"

"A diet for the lady and a regular for her date. Do you need a moment with the menu?"

"No, ladies first," he smiles at me. I almost want to ask for a plate of the Cory Koenig. No dressing.

"I'll take the shrimp linguine."

"I'll have the same," Cory winks at me and collects the menus to pass over.

"I don't have good taste in anything," I utter when Russ walks away.

"Not true, you're a Partisans fan. So, I had asked if you were seeing anyone."

Instead of trying to cover up my history, I opt to give him the now. "No, I was in a long term, but it didn't work out. You?"

"No, I'm not. I don't think it's a good idea to date in this career frankly. Too much moving around. No girl would want to go from Ottawa to Austin for me unless she only wanted my money. At that rate, I wouldn't want to date someone that didn't have a career and only relied on me. A little pathetic."

"Yeah, I feel ya. I hate women that think they'll get by on their looks. It's a very sad way to live life."

"I really admire you Jiles. It's cool as hell to meet a successful female comedian. I hope this is the beginning of a beautiful friendship."

Even if his words sound sweet as hell, I only concentrate on that one word. 'Friend.' Looks like I'm in the friend zone already. How the fuck did I do that?

**R**uss collects our plates and Cory tells me the hilarious story of the time he was mic-ed and accidentally shouted like a frat boy about advancing to the next round, not realizing everyone could hear his hooting. He's even more impressed when I tell him I know exactly what he's talking about.

"I love this, I'm so glad to know someone in town besides a teammate knows shit about the sport. This is going to be great, you can be there to console me when we don't make playoffs. It's going to be weird, having hockey end in April."

"You never know, maybe you'll bring the missing element to the ASS-assins."

"ASS-assins, I like it."

"Don't go using it at work, they'll get pissed I'm sure."

"Nah, they know I don't want to be here. It's kind of an unspoken rule that no one wants to play hockey in these hot weathered cities. So we all just fuck around about it. I'm probably going to be having some of the guys coming over for a party, you should stop by."

"That would be awesome, I'd love to meet more sexy hockey players," I admit before I realize I have said 'more.' At this point I hadn't breathed a word that I wanted him in that way. I don't want to ruin this calm dynamic.

"Sexy?"

"All hockey players are sexy. Even the ugly ones."

God, what a shitty save that was. I just made the ASS-assins goaltender look good.

"Oh, okay," he doesn't know what to say. Luckily, here comes back our little conversation saver Russ with our bill.

"Can I interest ya'll in any dessert? We have a fabulous tiramisu!"

"No thanks," Cory speaks for me, hoping to distance himself from the words I just uttered.

"Alright here's your bill," Russ sets down the slim black checkbook near Cory before walking away. Both of us reach into our wallets and toss our debit cards down on the book.

"It's on me," he insists.

"That's sweet, but I like equality. Next time you can have the whole bill. This is your first impression of me, and this is who I am. Someone who doesn't expect to get a free ride."

Now that save was reminiscent of a Bob Baker stoppage, Bob Baker being the long time goaltender of the Vancouver

Moose. I can sense the awe I've left in Cory's mind as he sees what kind of 'lady' I am.

"I like your style Perry," he puts both our debit cards in the check and props it up for Russ to fetch.

**W**e find ourselves outside of our doors after the horribly long walk up our 14 flights. A note on the elevator says it will be working again tomorrow, finally. If I wanted to exercise, I would join a fucking gym!

"I had a good time tonight Jiles. Thanks for showing me Austin."

"Are you kidding? This is nothing, there is far more to see. Did you know it's legal to be topless in Austin?"

"No kidding?"

"Yeah, but usually it's just women like me topless, no models or anything."

"Don't be so hard on yourself. So I'll let you know what's up with the party, okay? Would be cool if you met the team, they'd love to meet a hockey chick. I'm sure some of them are single."

"Eh, I'm not interested in dating, I've just got a big zam-boner," I say without thinking. Ah shit! This will ruin my chances with him.

"Oh?" he steps back an inch, raising just one of his eyebrows. No no baby, I didn't mean it!

"Well, I'm not against it. I just don't actively look for it. I'm not on the hunt for a marriage. When it happens, it happens."

"What's a zam-boner?"

"A hockey boner! A zamboni? I expect you would know what a zamboni is!"

"Of course. I just didn't pick up on your joke immediately. Well, I'll see you later then," he pushes his door open, giving me a final smile as he steps inside.

I close my door as well, confused as to what to do. I should find a distraction for myself before I start bitching about how stupid I acted and how I said all of the wrong things. But I think it's pretty clear he isn't interested in me. I take a seat and let out a groan. Then I do something I haven't done in a while. I turn on the TV and turn up the volume enough that I know Cory won't hear me.

And then I cry. Not because I know he's not into me. Not because of *Chrysler*. But because I know it will be a long time before anyone sees anything in me in ever again.

# CHAPTER 6

I managed to fall asleep in the midst of my tear fest on the sofa, waking up to my cell phone alarm at 5:30am. It takes me a few minutes to realize why I'm waking up this early before I quickly sprout up to throw on my clothes. Within 5 minutes I'm out the door and flying down I-35 back to the studio.

Ben, Mark and Dave welcome me in surprise that I didn't bail already.

"How'd you sleep?" Ben asks, taking a bite of his bagel a few minutes before the show starts.

"Decent, I should have gone to bed a bit earlier but I was out."

"On a date?"

"I wish."

"Who with?" he inquires. No way I'm going to tell him, I don't want him talking about this on air. It's a known fact that personal situations get told on this show and I don't want my sad attempt to fuck my neighbor known by all of Austin.

"Just some guy you wouldn't know."

The show goes better than yesterday because I knew what we were talking about beforehand, peppering in my trademark Jiles Perry comedy every chance I could. This is a great way for me to gain more fans, even if I can't be my usual extreme self on public radio. We gave away a pair of tickets to my taping via playing a round of the *Facebook* game. I managed to stay away from any relationship talk so no one in Austin knows about my sad exchange with Cory Koenig last night. I guess if I had talked about it, it wouldn't be the end of the world. That's because I just realized something: no one in Austin knows who Cory Koenig is.

"Seriously, who were you with?" Ben asks me as we walk to our cars.

"Let's talk over lunch, I'm hungry."

**B**en and I sit at *Whataburger*, a place where men and women go when they aren't trying to impress each other. Unless they're trying to impress each other with awesome burgers and chicken fingers!

"I have a new neighbor. He happens to be one of my favourite Ottawa Partisans who just got traded to the ASS-assins."

"Wow, that's huge. I'm sorry I don't care about hockey otherwise I might know who you're talking about. What's his name?"

"Cory Koenig. Ben, he is SEXY! And he's a red head, and you know how I love me some red heads. Man, he's like a deflated version of you! But I'm in his friend zone without even trying. Guys just don't look at me and see a regular woman. They see a friend. I guess it's my fault for not dressing like a woman."

"No it's not. Guys just think you're cool, and remember what Tim Tanning says? *"I don't fuck anyone I respect,"* he reiterates, complete with his own British touch.

"Touche. Is that why we never fucked?"

"Yes it is."

We dig into our chicken fingers and don't talk for the next 5 minutes, respecting our stronger need to eat then talk.

"This is why I love you Jiles. I can eat in front of you without feeling like a fucking pig," he plops another chicken strip into some white gray before slamming it down his throat.

"That's because I'm just as piggy as you. My body just happens to handle it better."

"Why didn't we ever go out?'

"I was with *Mitsubishi.*"

"I see you're catching on."

"Gotta move on somehow. Making fun of him seems to be the way to go."


After lunch we both go home for short naps. He explains to me that the only way to survive this early morning schedule is to pepper in a short nap afterward otherwise you drag on like a fucking zombie all throughout the rest of your day. I'm so lazy I fall asleep on the sofa in my clothes, waking up just in time for my daily dose of *Maury Show*.

"Who be da hoe now?" I repeat in midst of my laugh fest. Roniesha just found out Shamichael isn't the father of her two kids. Shamichael is so happy with this result. I feel bad for Roniesha, but seriously! Keep track of who you're fucking, eh? Keep a diary, or just post their names on twitter. No one will know why you're listing names and they will forever be listed on the internet for your logs. It will even have the dates too. Plus you can hash tag the name and see who else they've been fucking. Find out where your herpes came from.

Click, click, click. *"Shamichael be fucking my momma? GOOD LAWD!"*

Shamichael starts to do a funky break dance when I hear some laughter from the hall. I slowly turn my TV down just in case Cory can hear the quick hush of sound; I don't want him to know I'm an eavesdropper!

I listen as much as I can, going after another beer glass so I can in fact hear giggling coming from the living room: two pairs. A man and a woman. Aw fuck.

I listen as their voices trail from the living room to the bedroom. After about 15 minutes of waiting around, which I assume is them making out and taking off their clothes, the bed starts to rock. Slight muffled moans make it hard for me to determine who is who but I'm sure it's her, Cory seems modest and quiet. That cunt. That should be me in there. I wonder who she is, maybe the hostess? Maybe the server? Maybe it's just none of my business. I go back into the living room and get back to my show, trying to focus in on Maury's plight and not my own.

The show ends and I shut off the TV. I can hear them laughing again. It makes me sick to know how quickly some woman can be in his pants when he just moved in a few days ago. How could someone be such a slut? Then I remember how bad I wanted to fuck him, but wait! At least I know who he is. She just met the guy, and unless she's from Ottawa, I sincerely doubt she knew him prior to meeting. Geez, what if they just met today?

I decide I'll go for a quick ride around the lake on the ole tricycle, anything to get me out of this train wreck of thought. As I step into the hallway, I find that I am exiting my apartment at the very same moment as the fuckers.

"Oh hey," Cory says, feeling no shame whatsoever in his quick afternoon lay. It doesn't even take me a minute to see who is with him. She might be short, but she has no problem stepping in front to claim her territory. Women! I say these things like I'm not a woman too but quite frankly, I'm probably right.

"This is Vicki, she works for the Assassins."

"Oh? Cool. Not enough women in hockey," I say in the best attempt I can to sound sincere.

"Are you Jiles Perry?" she asks with quick recognition and not for the reason I want her to know who I am.

"Uh..." I stutter but Cory interjects.

"See Jiles, people totally recognize you. You're more important than I am in Austin!" he feels proud of this moment to bring fan to star, but he doesn't know the real reason why this woman knows me.

"Did you say Jiles Perry?" a voice comes from down the hall where a man has stepped out of the elevator. He's dressed in a suit and doesn't look like someone who would be a fan of mine. "You've been served," he hands me the file clearly marked with my fucking name on it.

As quick as he came, he leaves on the same elevator even. I must have been his quickest bust yet, busting faster than a virgin nerd who wins a chance to bone Pam Anderson.

Cory stares at me with a hefty mix of pity and inquiry. Tight lipped, I grimace and quickly unlock my door, slithering back into my apartment as fast as my unsteady hands can allow.

Humiliation is all I can even think about, never mind this serving. And I don't have to tell Cory why I'm being served. His new fuck will tell him for me.

I sit down beside my door and open the prong envelope. Divorce papers.

Instead of going out, I sulk back to my sofa and decide I'll just order in. I can't face the world now. I can't even face my damn neighbor. Thank god the morning show is at the ass crack of dawn when I can expect no one to see me on my way in or out. This early shift is better than I thought.

# CHAPTER 7

In 20 minutes I've made it obvious to myself that Cory is not going to bump into me again today. I know this because he's playing a game tonight! So I leave, still in what I wore to the show and go down to the nearest bar that serves the crafty beer I like. I sit at a high table that faces out the window so no one in the bar has to see me as I review the divorce papers. I don't understand what any of this legal shit means, it just means my ass is gone. I've never understood why the law has to get involved with people's marriages ending. I mean, having your husband leave you is bad enough. Do they really need to cake on lawyers, bills, confusing paperwork, and waiting in line at governmental offices where unfriendly employees will make you feel stupid if you don't understand what to do? Fuck me, America's treatment might be worse than my husband's.

I order a fancy brown ale titled *Big Sky Moose Drool*, which I order in honour of my moose dolls. I remember coming to this bar a few hours before I came home where *Lincoln Mercury* was sitting on the sofa with a dead expression, waiting to drop his shit bomb on me.

"Jiles, we need to talk," he reiterated like he'd been practicing all day long on how to do this. I guess everyone practices that line, mixing in just the right pinch of seriousness and also grievance. They need you to know how hard of a day they had rehearsing their *Oscar* worthy dump speech!

"What's up honey?" I said, taking a seat beside him.

Yeah, I called him lame shit like honey, baby, sweety moose.

"I won't dance around trying to give you a story so I'll just make it quick and simple."

He looked at me, took off his specs and presented me with the same look he gave me the day he told me his grandmother died.

"I'm leaving you."

"Huh?" my jaw dropped like a cartoon character. A sloppy, long armed frog comes to mind. Maybe this was an early incarnation of Reginald.

"I met someone else, and, I think she and I are meant to be together."

My bottom lip began to quiver and surprisingly enough I was able to fight back tears. I credit that with the beer I just had. It had numbed me to the point that I was in a state of utter shock instead of a sobbing little bitch. I'd never breathed so hard before, practically having to remind myself. You know how normally you just breath in and out and pay no attention whatsoever? This was one of those moments where I had to be in control of it otherwise I probably wouldn't.

"That's what you practiced all day long? That's the worst dump speech I've ever heard," I attempted to talk, trying to brush away the sincerity of this moment.

"Strong Jiles, always trying to make the best of a situation."

Why he said that, I had no clue. Was he going to try and

console me after he Hiroshima-ed me?

"I'm sorry. I loved the years we had together. We had memories I'll never forget babe. It's just that I feel like we lost our spark along the way, and this girl..."

"I don't want to know what you see in this cunt," I bitched. I didn't hold back my anger. My thoughts were going haywire, I knew I had no control of my word vomit.

"I'm sorry, I really am. It took a lot of balls for me to do this because it's so wrong and I know it with all of my heart. I won't ever stop feeling the way I do about you. You've been a huge part of my life. I just feel like, it's the right thing to do, and if that's how I feel, I need to live my life for me, not to make someone else happy."

Still in a hazy fucking cloud trying to make sense of all this without knocking his teeth out, I said nothing. His words were quite cold no matter how many times he said 'I'm sorry.' The beer helped me again, this time I heard music in my head. The blender heart song, by that band in the 90's. I decided I'd listen to *Eve 6* as soon as he was gone. I'd buy it on my phone from *iTunes* so I could listen to it on repeat at a bar while I got drunk.

"Jiles, I want you to keep the apartment. I'm the one leaving, I should have to move, not you. Besides, you can afford to take over the bills. You're a big star now, you're going to move on so fast your head will spin."

I didn't respond, I just tried so hard to make a lick of sense to what was sincerely going on. I let the time pass for a few minutes before I started again. My breathing was coming back to normal flow, but I could still feel my heart pounding against the rest of my empty soul.

"So you're leaving me?"

"Yes."

"I leave for my tour in just a month. It would have been a little bit nicer if you could have just messed around behind my back during the tour and then told me when I got back, instead of throwing this 100 pound suitcase of shit into my head when I'm going to go and make a career for myself."

"There's never a good time, Jiles."

"You're right, there's never a good time to start fucking someone else while you're married."

"You don't even want to have kids!"

"You said you didn't either!"

"I've grown up Jiles. Maybe you need to do that one day too. Instead you collect moose dolls and make a living talking about your sex life for money."

My body was fuming with this unnecessary insult. No one insults my moose!

"I have a sex life? I had no idea since you haven't fucked me in a month! What does she do? "

"I can't tell you."

"Why not? Is she a stripper?"

"It's just better in the long run if you don't know okay? I'm gonna go, this isn't good for you to argue right now."

"What the fuck would be good for me right now?"

"I don't know," he stood up, shuffled his feet and looked to the ground. "I'll have my things out while you're gone on tour okay?"

"Yup," I muttered, looking down at a random mark on the nice rug I bought at *IKEA*. God, what if it was a cum stain from his new girl?

"I'm sorry Jiles, I'll always love you," he said.

I looked at him as he tossed on a messenger bag and picked up two black hard shell suitcases sitting behind the sofa before making his way to the door.

When I felt my composure had enough in me to stand up, I carried my weight over to the terrace and had a seat. Now that he was long gone, it was time to let it all out. I cried harder than I ever knew I could to the point my eyes look so red it was as if I'd downed more pot than that *Snoopy Pooch* guy (I don't know what his name is but I know he smokes a lot) in a lifetime. I thank god no one can hear me next door since I'm now officially the only tenant on this floor. The only things I could think about were the emptiness I'd feel, the fear of repeated nights analyzing what nights I thought he was cheating on me, and for how long he'd been unfaithful. Then I remembered my tour and how it had been ruined. How I'd be able to be funny night after night with this on my shoulders, I'd never know. But I had to do it. It was clearly all I had left.

I snap out of my replay as I've finished my beer and decide I won't let that fucker get to me, I won't drink myself stupid because of him. And then a server asks if I'd like another beer and I say yes because I'm pathetic. I look up and see the Asses game is starting. I decide I'll watch the game and hope they lose.

**A**fter the game I pay my tab and head back up to my place. As soon as I get into my apartment, there's a knock.

"Why didn't you tell me you were getting divorced?" Cory asks when I open my door.

"Well hello to you too," I say, letting him inside. I take a seat at my island kitchen and he follows suit. "I figured it was a bit too soon to be admitting such huge portions of my life. Besides, no one wants to hear someone cry about their failed fucking marriage. I hate people like that. Don't divulge your whole life story to someone you just met. Ain't no one got time for that shit!"

"I feel horrible now for asking if you were single. I won't try to set you up with any of the players."

"No, it's okay. It happened before my tour, so I'm not all messed up in the head, crying my eyes out, eating bowls of poutine. I'm fine really."

"Yeah, maybe, but still. It must be horrible. And here I am rubbing my date in your face. I'm so sorry."

"I think I've met your date before," I admit. I need to know if she's told him.

"She knew you were getting divorced. It must suck to be so well known that people know of your affairs."

'Which affairs?' I wonder, but decide I'd like the information he knew ooze out of him like sloppy cum.

"Do you want to talk about it?" he asks. I admire his eyes once again and those small little lips that would make my skin relish in delight if they were anywhere near me. He stares at me like I'm one of Sara McLaughlin's dogs again, and I want to appease him so I start talking.

"I was married for a few years to my college sweetheart. He left me a month before I went on my tour. I don't know who," I lie. So not ready to divulge that information.

"Wow, that's horrible. It's all still fresh I take it. I'm so sorry."

"Don't be. Shit happens. I won't let it fuck with my career, because that's so much more rewarding than his."

"What does he do?"

"Finance. Came from money, but in the end I'm doing better than him. Maybe he left because he didn't like knowing I was outearning him. It used to be, Mrs. Richardson. But the more notoriety I got, the more it became Mr. Jiles Perry. His name was Ford. Ford Richardson."

"That reminds me of the Ford dealership in Ottawa," he laughs, then starts to sing the little jingle.

I bask in the familiarity of something only he and I would know. Something so rare to be in common with in Texas. This has to mean something good. I feel a tenderness across my table top and know he isn't going to let go of me any time soon. Maybe he needs a friend more than I need/want him.

"Do you find it hard to just drop everything and move to another city, let alone another country?"

"It wasn't so hard since I'm already from the US, but yeah. It's just rough. How do they think I can just drop my life in a day, say goodbye to my friends, my familiar haunts, and just begin again in a place so foreign to my element. I'm just thankful that there was a team waiting here for me. And you," he smiles earnestly.

"I appreciate that Cory. I'm glad you're here too. It's slightly comforting to know I'm not alone on this floor anymore."

"Do you wanna grab a late dinner? I just came home after dropping her off post game."

"She doesn't have a car?"

"She's 20," he says shyly, biting his cheek from within even.

I roll my eyes when he turns away. A 20 year old can get Cory Koenig (who like me, is 25) and a job with a professional hockey team? Fucking slut.

# CHAPTER 8

"So, yesterday I got served," I tell Ben over hot wings at *Pluckers*. His are hot, mine are mild. I'm a pussy. The place is empty after their lunch rush. I find it so nice to not be one of those people with an hour to eat, racing back to their offices before they get whipped by some asshole boss.

"Like, *Pineapple Express* served?" he asks.

"Yeah buddy. Seth Rogen, *'You've been served!'* served," I imitate. "It was so embarrassing because I was in the hall leaving and Cory and his date saw it. His date is a 20 year old, can you believe that shit?"

"Ooh, does she have friends?"

"Seriously Ben, you're not going to get a young girl in bed. You're no Cory Koenig."

"I could be a Cory Koenig," he gazes off, thinking how nice it must be to be a hockey player.

"That girl, she knew me. I'm so glad she had the decently not to tell Cory."

"Tell Cory what?"

"Okay Ben, I'm about to fuck you up with some truth. You know how I went from being a season ticket holder last year to absolutely despising the Austin Asses?"

"Yeah, I just figured you had better things to do that freeze your ass off."

"*Geo* left me for an ice girl."

Ben starts to choke on his wing, his fingers so smeared with red sauces that he can barely grab his glass of water. He finally musters it down his throat in a slushy mess, shaking his head in shock.

"You're fucking kidding me? He left you for a *Spice Girl*? Which one? *Scary Spice*?"

"Not a *Spice Girl*, an ICE girl. One of those stupid cheerleaders that has absolutely nothing to do with the grand sport of hockey."

"Oh, ice girl. Gotcha. Wow."

"Wow is right. I told him I wanted him to take an interest in hockey. I didn't mean take an interest like that. The bastard. I just can't go in there. I can't go to another game. I'm not even sure if I can go to the Partisans game. I can't watch her dance around. He probably goes to all of the games too now."

"I'm so sorry Jiles. What a fucked up thing to do. He knew how much you love hockey and he goes and totally ruins it for you, not to mention the whole fucking marriage."

Ben shakes his head in complete disdain, a new pity for me I've never seen. I always saw Ben as this guy who didn't care about other people's emotions, just the guy you tell your troubles to so he can make witty retorts back. Turns out I'm the funnier one when we discuss my divorce.

"I thought being Cory's neighbor would be great but now he's going to be bringing "dem" hoes to our building. His date was one of them. I know she's friends with that home wrecker."

"Don't let it get to you. You're Jiles Perry and they are nameless women dancing in swim suits in a freezing ice rink. At the end of the day, you're the *Stanley Cup*."

"Wow, you know what the *Stanley Cup* is?" I smile in complete guffaw. No one here knows anything about hockey. Not even the ice girls.

"I did some homework last night. Thought it might be cool if we went to a game together. But I understand if you don't want to go anymore."

"I might be able to stomach it. Just not yet."

"Does Cory know this?"

"No, he just knows I'm getting D-eed."

"Dicked?"

"Divorced. But I'm getting dicked too you could say."


It's another day of post radio/lunch with Ben that leaves me with nothing to do afterward so to pass the time I drink. I ran down to a local shop and picked up two six packs of *512 Pecan Porter*, so at least I'm at home this time. You might think I'm an irresponsible drunk, but at least I'm responsible enough to drink at home. I keep a trash can nearby in case I start hurling and can't make to the bathroom. See, I'm well prepared too.

I watch a marathon of *Saved By The Bell* on *TBS* and it's that episode where Jesse is addicted to some pills to help her get though her busy schedule. I wish I could say I'm busy so I have an excuse for drinking so heavily. When I've downed 6 episodes I decide I need to do something better than mindless loafing.

I go into my bedroom and lay down, getting into my moose footy pajamas. It's only 5pm but I know I have nothing better to do and I have to be up early. As I lay down and attempt to reclaim a comfortable position, I realize it's been almost 9 full months since I've had sex of any kind, I'm talking self too. I'm not really horny but at this pathetic realization I decide I'll have at me. I take off my jammies since there is no way I can conduct that ceremony in a tight one piece. I also turn my moose doll's heads away because I don't want them to watch me.

Just in a pair of undies and a lacy bra that I wear to impress myself, I slide my undies off and go feel around to see how turned on I am. Turns out, I'm already wet and I didn't even need to creep upwards for anything in the juice factory. I've never been one of those people to stick their fingers up there, that is so damn gross. It's so slimy and weird in there, I may as well jack off my nose while I'm at it.

I'm quite pleased with how wet I am so I start doing the damage that needs getting done. Emphasis on needs, it's been a while for poor ole me! I can't get anywhere for like 5 minutes which confuses me because I'm so wet, what the hell? Normally there is a reason I'm oiled up, but I cannot seem to find what it is.

Maybe I shouldn't have downed all of that beer, I think

to myself. I need some inspiration in the form of the Partisans. And inspiration comes along so fast it's almost like it's timed. Cory's bed's a' rockin'. That son of a bitch is getting laid again? I hope it's the same girl! But I can't jerk off to this because I want him and it would be weird. I already know there will be no 'oh' face so I get up to wash my hands before I put my clothes back on. I turn on the light in my master bathroom and scream like I've never screamed before. My fingers are red. I wasn't horny and wet... I started my period!

"AHHH!!!!" I shout as Reginald, jaw slamming down to the floor in horrific shock, my slimy eyes bogging out of my skull. I'm not sure if this sincerely applies since frogs probably don't have periods, but whatever. There is no earthly way to describe the mortified look on my face.

I scrub the crap out of my hand with more soap than I'd use for my body in a week before I decide I'm better off in the shower. It's fucking *Carrie* up in here but the joke is on me! *"They're all going to laugh at you!"* I scrub every inch of my body even if I know for a fact that it wasn't involved in what I could deem the world's biggest prank my body has ever pulled on me. You're a sly one, you little uterus you.

When I dry off and toss back on my moose jammies, I decide the only way to sweat off the humiliation is to have another beer. I take it to the patio and enjoy my view of the gorgeous downtown setting. Maybe it's a poetic moment in this setting, but I'm too far gone to appreciate it. I stare out as if I'm thinking intently when really I'm just lost.

Starting to cry a tad to myself, I hear the terrace opening. It could only be Cory since he is the only other resident on this floor. There's no way I can run off before he hears me so to play it cool, I keep quiet and decide I won't say anything unless he talks first.

"Hey Jiles, how's it going?" Cory says as soon as he sees me. I look over and watch him in his boxers and a plain white tee. He takes a seat in a lofty little chair with a beer of his own.

"Oh I've had better nights," I slur a tad, lazy eyed in my drunken daze.

"Are you drunk?"

"Oh I'm lit alright!" I laugh.

"Well at least you're home, good for you."

"I didn't want anyone to see me make an ass of myself. You on a date?"

"Yeah."

"Same chick?"

"Of course, I'm not a player," he takes a swig of his drinky drink drink.

"Playa," I say in a fake ghetto tone before slowly but surely I start to cry. Aw man.

"Hey, are you crying?" he takes a good look at me, standing up and getting as close as he can without leaping onto my terrace.

"No, I've just got something in my eye," I rub my right as if I'm looking for something that may have landed on my brown pupils besides the stream of tears that won't go away.

"What's wrong Jiles?"

"Nothing, I'm just stewing about my divorce. What other distractions could I possibly have? My life is damn good, I have no right to bitch."

"Jiles, it's totally okay to cry about your divorce. It's such a tough situation to face and I'm so damn sorry."

"What does everyone see in those girls huh?" I quickly turn into an angry drunk.

"What girls?" he asks naively. Oh come on Cory, we're on the same page here.

"*The Spice Girls.* So what if they have good music, they haven't put out an album shince (I slur) I grew pubes man. They all go dancing around in a goddamn swimsuit on an ice rink like it's a fucking career and everyone goes fucking gaga for them like they're the best thing they've ever seen. Guess what? There's just fucking humans too except their stupid humans! They're wearing fucking swimsuits on a goddamn sheet of ice and they are so cold their nipples poke and then everyone on the planet no matter how smart falls over themselves to fuck them. We don't do this shit in Ottawa man."

Oh fuck. Maybe I've said too much. Cory stays quiet but still eyes me. I know I've insulted the girl right behind his glass door but I'm too inebriated to feel sorry about anything I've said. All things considered, I've got every right to say this.

"Cory, you got here on Friday. A Friday! Guess what? It's Wednesday and you're already dating an ice girl! What did she do to you? What did you see in her that made you think you had to jump at that piece of ass NOW, huh?"

"Jiles, I think I'd better go," he sternly backs away and prepares to slide his smoggy glass door open. I imagine it's fogged from all of the hot sex he and his lil' hottie are having.

"Fine, go back to your girlfriend, your can't even drink legally piece of ass. Newsflash Cory, I'm your age and I'm a real fucking hockey fan, but I guess because I don't have a booty that suits the masses I'm never going to be good enough for people like you."

He goes back inside without another word. I know I've pissed him off and I bet if that girl overheard me, she's pissed too. Oh well. I push my feet against the ground in an attempt to stand up but I push too hard for my chair and instead end up slamming me and the chair all the way to the ground. I sit here for a moment as I rub the back of my head because I've slammed the top of my poor cranium on the concrete just slightly. Good thing I'm short, eh?

"Oww!" I moan and decide I'm too drunk to get up. So I sit here in all of my worthlessness and this is how I wake up at 5am. Good thing I have my cell phone in my pocket, alarm set for the show.

# CHAPTER 9

"Jiles, is it true your husband left you for one of the Austin Assassins Ice Girls?" a caller asks during another game on the Ben and Brodie show.

"Um, yeah. What does it matter at this point who knows? It was about half a year ago. I guess he saw a far better body than mine and decided he needed to move on. Good sleuthing for you, eh? Did someone update my *Wiki* page beside myself?"

"Alright, that's a wrap. Caller X gets the tickets, start ringin' those lines now!"

Ben furrows his eyebrows and purses his lips, horrified that a caller would ask such a personal question. He comes over and rubs my back, giving me a kiss on the cheek.

"I'm sorry Mark let that call through, I'm disgusted someone would ask you something so personal like that."

"No man, it's okay. Fuck, I'm just surprised someone knew! I guess I'm more famous than I thought."

"Still, not cool."

"What's not cool is how I acted last night. I got drunk and told Cory off about his 20 year old girl."

"What did you say?"

"I don't remember for sure, I just know I asked him what the hell everyone saw in those girls. I was so messed up that I accidentally knocked myself backward in my chair and fell asleep like that. Quite the interesting way to wake up in the morning, eh?"

"Haha, I'll say. You hungover?" Ben asks, flipping through paperwork to see what is next on the prize sheet for the last game of the show.

"A bit, I got superb at this during my tour. Where's lunch today?"

"How does BBQ sound?"

"Sounds better than most of the music this station plays. Seriously, stop playing this rap song. I don't care if a white guy wrote it, this is an alternative rock station!" I bitch when *Thrift Shop* comes on again today for the third time during the show.

E xpecting Cory to throw me a pity party for being a drunk loser (I'll do anything to spend time with him!) he instead has his own party. And the bastard didn't even invite me. I guess he really is still mad at me so I don't blame him. I pace around in my moose pjs debating if I'll go tell them to shut the fuck up, I have to be at work when the cocks crow. I might even be talking about Cory's cock, since he's obviously going to get laid tonight.

But, I don't want to be that neighbor. I want Cory to like me. Yelling at him is not the way to go. Besides, no one wants a neighbor that won't let you throw a party at your own convenience.

"I know Nicky, I'm pissed too," I tell my dead plant as I step onto my terrace. I look over at Cory's terrace and see a make out session in the works. It's some hot young thing and a guy I recognize, an Assassin. Ah geez.

I turn my plant the other direction as if it even has a head or a side that might be a head, then go back inside. I decide I'll suck it up and be a good friend to Cory. That is if we even are friends. I sure as hell want to know why I wasn't invited.

I lay there for maybe an hour with a pillow over my head for some peace and quiet but it just isn't working. Cory's party is too loud and I cannot sleep. No more Ms. Nice Neighbor.

Within seconds, Cory opens his door and looks at me with a bit of surprise. He's never seen my moose pjs before. I would feel embarrassed but I'm too pissed off to care.

"Hey dude could you turn down the music a bit? I have to be up at 5:00am every day this week."

"Fuck, why so early?"

"I'm filling in for Brodie on the Ben and Brodie Morning show this week."

"Oh I'm so sorry, I had no idea. Yeah I'll def turn it down."

Cory is about to close the door when I see a few girls sitting on his sofa. They're all looking at me with utter surprise, and unfortunately it's not because of my pajamas.

"Nice pjs!" one of the girls calls out to me. What a cunt. I flip her off and storm back to my place. I don't care if Cory hates me now. I just know I hate his pussy posse.

I go back to my place and jump in bed, immediately hearing the music turned down. Suddenly I'm regretting this move, because now I'm overhearing their conversation.

"Was that Jiles Perry?" a woman says loudly. Crap, do they really think I can't hear them?

"Yeah, are you guys fans? She's pretty cool," Cory asks.

"Wow, what are the odds of that. She must hate you!"

"Why would she hate me? She loves hockey."

"You don't know about her ex-husband?"

"Yeah, so?"

"Her husband left her for Katie."

"Who is Katie?"

"One of the ice girls, she's probably the hottest on the team. Jiles used to have season tickets and now she never shows up anymore."

"God, did you see her pajamas? No wonder Ford left her!" one of the bitches chimes in her two cents.

I overhear the girls laugh again. I think about downing a few beers or even a few sleeping pills to rub this hurt off of me, but fuck them. This is my apartment, my job schedule, and...I'm outta here. I grab my pillow and some clothes, then throw them into my Partisans gym bag that has never seen a gym. As I'm closing the door behind me, Cory steps out of his place. We have good timing, eh?

"Jiles, I'm so sorry, I had no idea," he says, even reaching out to grab my hand. I pull away and keep walking, trying my best to stifle my tears as I march forward to the hopefully working elevator. It isn't, goddamnit! I don't want to walk back passed him to go down the stairs; I don't need another awkward moment. In the short span of my contemplation, I turn around, start walking casually and as soon as I'm in front him again, I whip out my best *Curly* impression.

*"Woob woob woob woob,"* I say while I glare at him and toss in the classic hand push too.

I drive to Ben's place on the east side and knock on the door in my moose pjs and sneakers.

"Jiles, what's wrong?" he rubs his eyes, clearly in the middle of his own siesta.

"Can I spend the night?" I ask, holding up my pillow and bag.

Without speaking, he puts his hand around my waist and ushers me inside, closing the door behind himself.

"What happened?" he asks as I climb in alongside his king size bed. He pats the space beside him for me to get closer.

"Cory was having a party and there were tons of those

ice girls there. I asked him if he could lower his music and they saw me from the hall and started talking shit. I could overhear those cunts through the wall making fun of me for fuck sakes! Not in my own goddamn home man, enough is enough."

"Those girls are awful," he sympathizes, grabbing my hand beneath the sheets. "I promise, I will never ever fuck an ice girl, no matter how hot they are."

"Thanks Ben," I roll over to face him. He gives me a kiss on the cheek and we fall asleep facing each other. Something about this is more comfortable than any nap I've ever taken with *Audi*.

# CHAPTER 10

"Why don't you have hockey boy come on the show Friday for the sports segment?" Ben asks me as soon as we take our chunky headphones off. I quickly feel the sweet release of the tension from around my ears. My head must be massive compared to Brodie's, that thing is way too tight on my melon.

"Say what? You know people in Austin don't care about hockey!"

"Yeah well, he's the closest we're gonna get to an actual athlete, so bring him in okay?"

"I'll do my best to convince him. If you think I'll sleep with him to get him on the show, then you're right."

Post morning show I come home to find Cory's door open. As soon as I pass by, he's out and walking beside me like an eager child following mommy home from school.

"Hey, can we talk?" he asks.

"Uh, sure," I say, knowing full well what this will entail. I unlock my door and let him in, walking him to the sofa as we both sit down. I'm still hurt about last night, but I know it's not his fault so I shouldn't take it out on him.

"Why didn't you tell me?"

"About what?" I try to play off. I don't want him to know I could overhear them talking.

"That your ex left you for an ice girl. Is this why you hate the Assassins?"

"No, I hate them because their fans are annoying yuppies who know nothing about hockey. They probably just cannot afford football games so they bring that lame mentality to hockey and think they know what's up when they don't know shit!"

"Jiles."

I blow smoke, I mean breathe out long and hard, lowering myself back in my seat. Fine, I'll tell him the truth.

"It's a big part. I used to go to a lot of games because I just wanted to see hockey. It didn't matter who was playing, you know?'

"I'm sorry Jiles, I had no idea. I don't know who that girl is, and honestly I hope I never do. I might punch her in the face. I'm sorry about those girls last night, I didn't really know them, my girl just invited them over. I didn't appreciate their attitude at all. And about the night before, I totally understand now why you said what you said. You're right, I am moving way to fast with her. I guess like your ex, I'm an idiot who falls for girls like that."

I don't know what to say to this. Neither does he.

"How did it happen?" he asks.

"I don't even know. I guess you could say it's my fault,

because I started taking him to hockey games. I wanted him to share my love for the sport. And then when I started doing small tours, I guess he got a little more involved than I wanted. I came back from a show in Dallas and he sits me down and says he's leaving. He told me he had met someone else but he didn't say who. I found out for myself later because I saw them together and recognized her immediately. She always seemed to stick out on the jumbo tron during those ridiculous dance numbers that have nothing to do with hockey during intermission. Jumbo tron, more like jumbo tits."

"You must hate me for bringing home an entourage of them."

"Hey, they aren't all bitches. Don't stop being their friends or inviting them over because of me, please. It's your life. I'm sure some of them have a heart."

"The girl I'm seeing, she's sweet. She admitted to me later that she knew, but it wasn't her place to tell me your business."

"That was nice of her," I admit, pushing out my lips in a jut, feeling my nose with my upper lip. For someone that talks for a living, I feel at a total loss of words around Cory.

"And I'm sorry I didn't invite you, I just thought it would be awkward after your drunken speech. Next time you should totally come over, it would be the greatest ultimate fuck you to those girls if you hooked up with a player."

I start laughing hysterically, slapping my leg even. Cory doesn't seem to be clued in.

"Dude! You were with a pack of ICE GIRLS and you

think a hockey player would hit on me?" I point with such enthusiasm for what an absurd remark that is.

"Hey, don't be so hard on yourself. Why are you so negative? You're not ugly."

"Come on man. My first everything left me for one of those girls. I know what they look like and I know what I look like. I'm no Avril, I'm an Alanis. Not that Alanis is ugly, but she's no Avril!" I quickly decide to defend Alanis. One day she may be my pal!

"Is this what your act is about, you joking on yourself?"

"It sure is. I have to beat people to the punch about me. Otherwise it might hurt those things, what are they called?"

"Feelings?" Cory tosses in.

"Yeah, those."

"Well, at any rate I feel pretty bad. But how is this morning show thing going for you?"

"Oh it's great. My good friend is the host of the show, Ben White. I went to college with him so he generally calls me up when he needs a show fill in. He knows I'll get up early as fuck because I clearly have nothing else to do. By the way, Ben wants to know if you could come on the show tomorrow during the 9am hour for sports, ya know, talk about the sport no one in town gives a rats ass about," I still hesitate for the idea. Something tells me Ben has a trick up his sleeve than just wanting to talk hockey, a sport he knows nothing about.

"Oh yeah? That would be cool. Sure, just give me the

address and I'll try my best to wake up early," he gleefully accepts. Cory knows the amounts of press here will be about 1% compared to the constant media hounding of Ottawa. He'll take what he can get.

"You can wake up early. If I can do it, you can. After all, I major in laziness and slobbery. You're an athlete, I know you're above me."

"If beating yourself down has bought you fame and fortune, I suppose it's for the best. When is your show by the way?'

"In a couple of weeks."

"Great, I'll be there."

"Seriously?"

"Yeah, why not. But under one condition," he stands up, looking down at me like a naughty dog who shit the carpet.

"What's that?"

"You have to come to an Ass-assins game."

"Cory," I shake my head fiercely in opposition. So strongly in fact that my hair whips around my face and that hurts!

"Come on, you know you love hockey. Don't let one person ruin your favourite sport. You're a Canadian, you know you have to get over it eventually."

"I know, I know. What game?"

"Next Friday. We play Vancouver."

"I'll go, only because I love Baker."

"Alright, I'll get you a seat behind the bench, and I'll get you in downstairs so you can meet the guys."

For a moment, the sweet idea of meeting the Vancouver Moose makes me wonder why on earth I hesitate, but it slowly dawns on me that I will have to face the most dangerous street gang in Austin, the Ice Girls! Lead by their master pimp, MacDaddy Ford.

The idea of this makes me want to jump to the ceiling and swing around on my ceiling fan like a cat about to fall into a pit of water.

# CHAPTER 11

I sit in the studio glancing down at my clock, watching the minutes display 9:00 a.m. Cory is supposed to be on at 9:20 a.m. I quickly fear he will bail out on me, which is generally appropriate when it comes to hot guys and me. But this isn't a date!

"Where is he Jiles? I already said he'd be on the show last hour!" Ben snaps which frightens me. He's a big guy after all. He taps his fingers rhythmically on the desk, looking around with an icy glare for the moment the door will burst open.

"He said he would be here," I whimper, looking at my text messages to see that he hasn't responded to anything I've sent.

"Sorry I'm late!" Cory says as he enters the room. Thank heaven! I can tell he's tired, which I do feel for him since we are both pretty lazy when it comes to the wee hours of the day. I see an exhausted expression on his face as he takes a seat beside me. He hasn't even looked up to introduce himself yet.

"So you're the infamous neighbor?" Ben asks him, reaching his hand out across the desk.

"I am. And you must be Ben White," he smiles, shaking in return.

"We will have you on in about 20 minutes, you can tell

us about your thoughts for the upcoming season, some of the scheduled games, and maybe what changes have been made to the Assassins line up."

After a quick news segment, the sports intro sounds and I see Ben with a glimmer in his eyes. I can see he's going to do something mean, but I'm not sure exactly what.

"We'd like to welcome to the show, the Austin Assassins' Cory Koenig, traded from Ottawa in the off season. Good morning Cory."

"Good morning guys, thanks for having me."

"Well, we couldn't get anyone else on our lousy ass show. So, tell us about the upcoming season!"

I already don't like Ben's comment. I know he doesn't like hockey but that doesn't give him a right to treat Cory like he's not a professional.

"It just started actually and we've won our first two games. We've got a great new coaching staff. The Assassins really changed their line up to add more offense to their roster. I was traded for Paradise and Shooter since Ottawa needed better defense. Our first two games went great, we're hoping to slowly build momentum for our first playoff appearance in a good 5 years."

"Yeah yeah, so tell me Cory. Why won't you date your neighbor, our co-host Jiles?"

I quickly feel the seething flames of my embarrassment swallow me up. Ben holds this stupid smirk on his face, avoiding eye contact because he knows one look at me and I will make him spontaneously combust. Cory looks quite dumbfounded himself, looking at me and wondering why this has turned so personal.

"Uh, excuse me?"

"It seems like you're keeping Jiles awake with an ice girl. What do you see in those girls that you don't see in my best friend?"

"Ben, I don't know what you're talking about. I live in Pflugerville and we all know Cory is a baller living in a mansion in West Lake!"

"Jiles is a great girl, she's been through a lot of crap but she actually loves hockey. I figured a professional player would rather take up a true fan than a girl who pretends to like hockey for money."

I'm so humiliated I could almost start crying. Cory's face is red, but certainly not redder than mine.

"I don't think discussing who I date on your so called 'lousy' show is appropriate and I don't think your bosses would like it when they find out you treated your guest to such nosy questions."

"I notice you're a red head," Ben quickly changes the subject. He doesn't like that threat.

"Yeah, I see you and this guy here are as well," Cory says as he points to producer Dustin.

"And this guy here, he's 28 and bald," Ben points to Mark when he happens to come in the room at just the right moment. Mark rolls his eyes and takes a seat in the corner. "So, you don't want to talk about your dating life, tell us where you're from."

"I'm from Detroit and I played for the Manitoba farm team in Winnipeg before my long stint in Ottawa."

"Detroit huh?" Ben snickers. He loves to make fun of Detroit.

"What's wrong with Detroit?" Cory asks.

"Ha! What's not wrong with Detroit?"

"Have you even been there?" Cory eyeballs Ben with mad furiosity.

"No I haven't. I don't want to get shot."

"Well then, don't judge a book by its cover. I'm sure being a fat ass and all, you'd hate it if no girls gave you the time of day based on what they saw and not who you are.

"Touche my friend," Ben applauds him for his witty comeback. "How did Detroit do for you?"

"Detroit treated me just fine. After all, my participation in Michigan youth hockey got me to a million dollar job where gorgeous women throw themselves at me all the time. I highly doubt you and producer boy here will make that much money in a life time. And I'm sure women don't flock to you at remotes where you give away koozies."

"You're still a ginger, it's not that easy," Ben says. "But it's easier than being bald," he jokes at Mark as well. Mark is seething too, he's quite sensitive about being bald. I know from years of being a fan of the show that Mark will quickly throw a temper tantrum. I'm waiting for one now.

"So we should start the gingers club of Austin," producer Dustin chimes in to erase the still brewing tension in the room. It's so hot in here. Did the AC go out?

Ben looks at the screen to read a message from the show's most loyal listener. "Ray in San Angelo says we could start a boy band called Soulless II Souless."

"If you guys start a gingers of Austin club, I wanna be president. I could have all of the guys to myself since everyone thinks gingers are gross but me apparently," I comment.

"I'd rather be ginger than bald!" Ben pokes Mark again.

Mark stands up like he's about to leave, then quickly turns around with bogged out eyes directed at the leader of the pack.

"Let me tell you something Ben! I may not have any hair but at least when I did my hair color wasn't gross looking and my skin is still a sexy tan that you will never obtain! So what if I'm bald and 28? You're a fat ass and Dustin here is a total dorko with his *Batman* shoes and this guy here? Hockey in Austin? Why don't you just bring curling while you're at it too, EH? I've had it with you guys, and I've even more so had it with these stupid interns! I said save the file! Save the damn file before you close the window, otherwise you have to make the damn podcast of the episode all over again! I don't get paid enough to deal with all of you morons! And why don't any of the buttons work? Why is Ben getting paid like Oprah but we can't afford a computer from 2005?!"

Mark slams the door as he exits. We all sit silently,

stunned at this while predictable, still awkward outburst.

I lean into the microphone and speak up. "Next time on the BALD and the Beautiful."

The room erupts with laughter and I see Ben wink at me for saving the show from that hideously awkward outburst.

"Jiles Perry ladies and gentlemen," he drums my name up while playing a sound bit of fake applause. And this time it works!


"**W**hat the hell was that?" Cory asks me as soon as we get outside where his car is parked beside mine.

"I have no idea, I'm so sorry. I'm really embarrassed. I'll definitely talk to Ben about this."

"Is there something going on here Jiles? Are you hiding something else from me? God knows you won't tell me shit unless someone else tells me first!"

He's right. I haven't been up front about a single thing. But why would I tell him that I like him now? Now that he knows what a fuck up loser I am. I can't say, "I want to date you," to a man whose blue eyes are looking back at me with the glisten that only an iced donut can make me yearn for.

"He's just trying to help me move on. I guess he hates the ice girls for hurting me."

"You can't blame everyone for one person's mistake Jiles! I have nothing to do with it and neither does my girlfriend! I'm not coming on this show again," he nods his head, tossing off the embarrassment on his shoulders as he gets into his vehicle.

I go back into the studio and find Ben watching porn on his *iPhone* with Dustin. I snatch the snatch on his phone out of his hand and throw it to the floor.

"How could you humiliate me AND Cory like that?" I shout, my hands on my hips like I'm sassy or something.

"Jiles, I was just trying to do some investigative research as a journalist!" he avoids eye contact with me, clearly not taking my pain seriously.

"This isn't funny Ben! Cory is totally pissed off at me! I'm so embarrassed."

"I know, I'm sorry Jiles. I guess I just saw him and wondered why on Earth he doesn't see all of the amazing things I see about you. I had to know why, and I guess my brain was too frazzled to wait until after air to ask."

"Ben," my expression does not change. I'm waiting for Ben's face to show any amount of remorse. He's a good talker, after all. I need sincerity.

"It's not an excuse. I really am sorry. That was lame as hell of me."

"You're lucky it's Friday, I'm done helping out."

I quickly turn my back to them and leave the studio, hoping that no one in Austin was tuned into those few moments that my dirty laundry was subtly pushed out for everyone to hear. I'd rather they see my actual dirty laundry: poop stains and beer spills.

# CHAPTER 12

"Can I take you on an apology lunch?" Ben texts me as soon as I get home. I wait until a few hours have passed to say yes. Not because I want to torture him, but because I fell asleep.

"Make it a good meal," I write back. "Better than fast food."

"Meet me at *Quatros* at 2pm."

I enter right on time to find Ben sitting at a table in an Assassins shirt. Who knew they made XXXL? Just kidding. He's an XXL.

"Why are you wearing that horrible shirt?"

"To show you that I care about hockey, and you," he pouts, pursing his lips in a sympathetic little smile. "My mom even called me after the show and yelled at me. She said she could sense tension in the room."

"Good for her."

"I made a huge mistake. I'm overprotective of you, kid. I don't like people hurting you. I should have waited until later to say something."

"You don't need to say anything to him!" I try to shove this theory down his already filled throat.

"Alright! I won't interfere. Are you serious about not being on the show anymore?"

"I thought Brodie was coming back in on Monday?"

"She is. But the boss wants to know if you could fill in for Melvin on Monday and Tuesday next week. He does the 6-10pm slot, it's basically just music and giving out tickets via no games. No fun in my opinion, but they really liked you on the show."

"Oh yeah? Sure, why not? I have nothing better to do. I will just need a quick rundown of the buttons."

"No problem-o, I don't mind joining you for night one. We could make it a slumber party and fuck under the desk."

"I'm sure plenty of interns have beaten us to that."

"They were going to ask Mark to do it, but they heard his work last night and they like you the non 94X employee better."

"That bad?"

"He sounds like *Kermit the Frog* to be exact, over enunciating just about everything he says."

"Has he simmered down?" I ask, quickly recalling Mark's meltdown.

"Simmered down? He's always like that! The guy just needs to vent a little and he happens to do it at the worst times when everyone can hear it. I don't blame him, those interns are pretty annoying. Annoying in that they are hot but won't bang us."

I laugh at this well played joke. Ben is pretty damn funny himself. He and I should be the new *Sonny and Cher*. Ben would never die in a skiing accident because Ben is lazy and would never do sports. And me? Me too.

"If it's at night do I need to be G rated or can I be myself?"

"Try to be G rated, if you slip up, there's a delay. As a thank you, next week let's go float the river, and I've got us some tickets to see the greatest band in Texas!"

"You got *Toadies* tickets?" I light up like a Christmas tree at a store display minutes after midnight on Halloween.

"Heck yes I did! It's *Dia Le Los Toadies*, did you forget?"

"I did actually. That's awesome, thanks man. Finally, something to look forward to besides the peepshow I have with my neighbor."

"Peepshow?"

"I can hear him fucking. Well, I can hear her and the bed shaking. So unless Cory shakes his bed and moans like a woman when he jacks off..."

"Can I come by and listen?"

"Sure, just don't jack off in my bed."

"Shucks," he snaps his fingers before tossing a few small fries into his mouth. He's almost cleared his plate, but

I've got half to go. I'm a pig too but I can't eat as fast. "What are you doing this weekend?"

"Nothing, honestly. I have no fucking life, you know this."

"Me neither, I'm doing a remote tonight at *Pluckers*, giving away some *ACL* badges and whatnot. You wanna come with?"

"Sure, what do I need to do?"

"Be charming and cute," he smiles and gives me a thumbs up.

"Well I guess I'm uninvited."

"**J**iles, why are you wearing those pajamas again?" Ben asks when he comes inside and finds me getting situated with a bottle of pop and some snack-eroos for the night of fun. It's time for him to teach me the ropes of hosting the night time slot. He's dressed down in his usual ensemble: an old pair of faded cargo shorts and some giant sneakers topped with a burnt orange UT shirt.

"You said it would be like a sleepover," I defend while scooting some of my loot over to his side of the desk.

"Well shit, if I knew we were going this casual I would have came in my pajamas. Better known as my birthday suit."

"Your suit is so big I wouldn't be able to see your dick."

Ben grits his teeth at me for a second before I see a light bulb go on in his head.

"Got something funny to say?" I inquire.

"Something fun for the end of the night. We're on in a minute, get ready. I'll do buttons for the first hour until you get the flow of this shift and then I'll show you the tricks."

We both place our giant headphones on and take hold of the mics. I see Ben nod his head as he thinks to himself.

"Good evening ladies and gentleman, this is Ben from the Morning Show and guest co-host Jiles Perry filling in for Melvin tonight. He's out getting some surgery so send him some tweets of support."

He points to me and lets me know it's my turn to speak.

"We've got a fun evening lined up for you of prizes and plenty of the best in new alternative rock music. We'll start out the night with *Queens of the Stone Age, Smooth Sailing*."

I quickly pull the headphones off as does Ben. "Is this seriously it?"

"Pretty much. It's pretty boring to be honest. Actually, at the rate I cum I could masturbate between every song and never get caught by the higher ups," Ben laughs. I wonder if he laughs at his ridiculous statement or the fact that he holds no shame in admitting his quick shortCUMings to me.

"Knock yourself out buddy, I don't care," I snicker, leaning back in my posh reclining seat. These chairs are probably the most upscale part of this entire studio.

"No way! I'm not jerking off in front of you Jiles."

"Geez, you act like I'm a girl or something. It's not like anyone would see you beside me."

"Hey! How about you..." Ben starts to laugh and hides his face for a minute. I wonder what he's cooking up. "Those things have a trap door, you should totally dance around with your ass showing."

"Why the hell would I do that?"

"If you're gonna see me jerking off, you gotta shake that ass. I gotta get it up some how!"

"Oh geez," I roll my eyes. Men and their obscenity. Ben might be the only person I know that's more crass than me.

"Hey, it's a 50/50 bet."

"I don't wanna see your dick that bad Benny."

"I don't really care to see your ass. I'm just saying, if I'm gonna do something stupid, so should you. Come on, it will help the time go by. We can do stupid dares between commercial breaks."

"Okay, I'll do it during the next one. But that means you have to jerk it in the next one."

"Scouts honour," he salutes me. We toss our headphones back on as the song comes to a close.

"Get ready to call in for our first pair of tickets to see Buffalo Speedway, November 19 at *Stubbs BBQ*. Caller 94 gets the tickets."

Ben thinks for a split second and decides to give out some more info, none of which I'm familiar with.

"And also, you can check out our website and find the ass of the night. I repeat, get on our website and find the ass of the night. The first person that calls in with the keyword gets a special prize."

"Ass of the night?" I ask when the commercials start.

"It's a new promotional thing we're doing. Don't worry, it's only on Monday nights. Something weird Melvin started."

"Uh, okay."

"Well, it's commercial break time. Get moving Jiles!"

I stand up with a bit of shyness. Even if I'm pretty much willing to do a lot of shit for fun, the idea of dancing with my ass showing in front of Ben seems weird. He's never seen me in the nude!

"Oh yeah, pull them pants down baby," he laughs at me as I unbutton the trap door of my moose pjs. "I promise, you are not the first ass this room has seen."

"I believe it! I was listening the week Brodie posted the image of your ass on *Facebook*."

Ben pulls up the big butts song from his own cellular device and I start dancing away like the fool that I am. Ben is laughing harder than I expected. I didn't think my horrid dancing was that funny, but Ben's face is turning as red as his hair.

"Twerk it!" he says after another minute of my Tom Foolery.

"I don't know what that means dude, I'm not cool."

"Then just shake your booty."

"Dude, it's not that funny," I manage to mutter while I boogie down.

"Okay okay you can stop now, we're almost back on," he squeaks out. He's got tears rolling down his face. "Get ready to answer the phone."

I pull up my undies, put my trap door back up, put my headphones back on, and have a seat as the 'On Air' sign lights up.

"Caller 11, your on. You didn't win the Buffalo Speedway tickets but DID you find the ass of the night?" Ben inquires to the first call that he answers.

"Well I found the bare ass on the 94X webcam if that's what you meant? Jiles' ass?"

My eyes grow larger than my breasts could ever be. My mouth drops. "Wha?"

Ben begins laughing again, to the point he can't even speak straight. He's puffing and wheezing like an old hobo on the street that somehow always manages to get a cigarette.

"Uh, yeah, you found the ass of the night but I would say the real ass of the night is Ben White. Stay on the line to claim your prize. Keep on trying to be caller 94 so you can get a pair to see the amazing Buffalo Speedway at *Stubbs*, November 18."

"BEN!" I glare at him, slamming my hand down so hard on the desk that it hurts me even. "What the fuck was that guy talking about?"

Ben says nothing; instead he wipes his laughter tears away and turns his laptop to face me. It's on the 94X website. And there's a....no fucking way....there's a webcam facing me.

"WHAT THE FUCK IS GOING ON?!" I shout like *Stu* in the *Hangover* when they first get attacked by Leslie's goons. I jump out of my seat, forcing my roller chair backward.

I forget the extra durable corded headphones are on my head and it pulls me so hard down toward the table that I slam my head on the desk. As if that wasn't enough, I bounce back while the headphones finally fall off. Now that nothing is holding me down while I ricochet around like a ping pong, I land with my back on the floor, all the while Ben is laughing even harder than when I was dancing. He's laughing so hard we can't even hear the music or the ringing phones.

There's no way I'll get up in my moment of shame. I see a remote of some sort beside me on the ground and chunk it, aiming for Ben's crotch. I guess all of my failed attempts to play darts and those rigged carnival games were all just adding up to this one precious moment where I finally get my bulls eye. I hear Ben yelp and his laughter is cut off completely.

"Congrats to caller 94, you're going to see Buffalo Speedway. And for those of you feminists, Jiles' just got me in the ball sack. I'm done laughing."

I finally come up. I sit back down and flip off the webcam.

"Time to nut up, beotch!" I tell him off air.

[A/N:See the real video at Vanessaloveshockey.com]

# CHAPTER 13

It's Tuesday night and I'm manning the studio myself, which is kind of a big fucking honour to me seeing how 94X is one of the premiere stations in Austin and they apparently trust me, the local jest, to handle all of this. The clock is ticking toward 6pm and the previous host is ready to get home.

"Good luck tonight," he pats me on the back on his way out. I toss on the chunky headphones and get comfortable in the seat, inhaling the hot coffee I grabbed for free from the community kitchen. I know I can afford *Starbucks venti* but fuck it, free is free, no matter how rich one may be.

I watch as the clock ticks and my time is on as soon as the promo starts up.

"Good Tuesday evening guys, this is Jiles Perry, local Austinite and comedian on the rise filling in for Melvin tonight, he'll be back tomorrow from a quick surgery recovery. I'll be here for four hours tonight, long enough for a guy to attempt to bring a chick home or two if they're any good. Then again trolling for pussy on a Tuesday is kind of pathetic, and it's early."

I realize what I've said and quickly hit the delay button. Whoops!

"Ignore that! Good thing I'm not an actual employee. We've got *ACL* passes to give away on the hour every hour so caller X gets the tickets and when I answer, don't ask me what I bleeped out. Please. Next up, *Phoenix*!"

A song starts to play and the phones start ringing. I answer as fast as I can to let each caller know whats up. I make someone very happy by telling them they are caller 94 which grants them 2 badges to weekend one of *ACL* next month. I answer the next few calls to let them know the contest is over before everything gets quiet again. The phone rings a few minutes later.

"94X," I say.

"Jiles, did you bleep out pussy?" Ben asks with a hearty laugh.

"Uh...yeah. Why are you listening?"

"Hey, I had to hear your first attempt. All in all, good job, you got me to laugh."

"Thanks man! And by the way, I've had like 20 people write me on *Facebook* thanking me for my ass dance so I kinda fucking hate you right now."

"But did your *Twitter* followers go up?"

"By about a thousand."

"You're welcome."

I hang up and look at what songs are up next. I'm excited when I see my new song on repeat is going to be on, *Eve 6's "Inside Out."* I know it's an old song, but I've just finally started paying attention to the lyrics and I enjoy them wholeheartedly. Plus the lead singer happens to be a sexy ginger, and I love gingers oh so much! Truth be told, he even looks a little like Cory too.

The song starts up and I decide to sing along. But first I toss my hoodie over the webcam.

*"I would [don't wanna get sued],*
*I would [don't wanna get sued]*
*But the [don't wanna get sued]*
*I would [don't wanna get sued]*
*Heart in [don't wanna get sued]*
*Ren[don't wanna get sued]"*

I'm so into it I even jump up and dance around. I'm rocking out so hard and at this point I'm so happy no one is else is in the studio. This song so speaks out to me, I completely identify with the shit *Toyota* put me through.

*"I don't want to get sued but you know what lyrics I'm singing!"* I sing at the top of my lungs as the song ends. I sit back down in my seat completely out of breath then realize I need to talk in 5 seconds.

'On Air' goes back on and I speak.

"You should have seen how terribly I just danced and sang along in here, that song might be old but man did it make me feel alive! Now everyone's favourite rap song on the rock station!"

I roll my eyes at the next track and take my head phones out. Not listening to that shit.

**M**y fill in period is over and with my 7 day stint working as a radio DJ, I decide I will celebrate with some drinks, even it it means by myself. You might call me an alcoholic, and you're probably right.

"Hey Jiles," a female bartender waves at me as I plop in at an empty table. I wave back even though she'd made it look like I drink too much, I actually know her because she used to do open mic night too.

"Can I get a stout?" I ask the perky server, perky because her nipples are poking through the thin material of her pink tank top. It's a tad chilly in here, that's what happens in a Texas summer. To compensate for the hot hot hot temperatures, we have to make sure every AC is at 40, making everyone uncomfortable no matter where they are. I wear my Ottawa jersey to keep warm and brush my hair out my face before I bottoms up into my fresh glass. It's karaoke night at this bar, which seems like the worst tactic ever to bring people in on a Tuesday night. I see a girl go up in a low cut outfit and I wonder what hideous occasion has happened to make her dress this way. It takes me about 2 more seconds to recognize the logo on her outfit, she's a goddamn ice girl. Seriously?! On the bright side, it's no occasion, it's her daily routine.

She starts singing some horrid pop song and I can't tell which diva plays the song otherwise I would have told you already with a side dish of a good mean joke. Our little performer makes sure to include all of the moves she can, winking into the audience while blowing kisses. I look into that direction and realize she's doing all of this to my neighbor.

Cory looks over in my direction, maybe to avoid eye contact in his own pool of embarrassment. His eyes light up a little, probably because I'm the only other person in the room who isn't impressed with her slutty number. He motions for me to join his table, so I reluctantly move over.

"Hey," he says without being too loud that people can recognize he's not watching his girl.

"This is so fucking stupid," I blurt out.

"Thank you, I'm probably not allowed to say those words," he snickers, a sheepish pout now erased from his tender lips.

"Does she wear that outfit everywhere she goes?" I ask.

"More than she needs to. I think it's a dumb way to get attention, but she looks great in it. She's really a nice girl, I just wish the vanity would float away."

"If it floats away there would be nothing left," I chirp in with my own mimicking wink and thumbs up. Cory can't help but laugh at my mean spirited comment. I feel that since we've established why I hate ice girls, I'm completely allowed to make any comments about them that I please, even if I am insulting the girl he's seeing. Deep down he probably would make the same joke too, he's just too much of a nice bro to say so.

"Oh I heard about your video," Cory reveals to me. I was riding high on the idea that I had new followers. But this? Oh man. Ben is so dead.

"I'm so humiliated. I had no idea there was a webcam in there."

"One of the guys on the team sent it to me. I guess someone was able to hack the thing and now it's on *YouTube*. It had about 5,000 views when I watched it this morning."

I start choking on my booze to the point I spit up on the table. I feel like a baby, one that has goober (whatever that shit is called) all over its chin and spitting up. The baby wallows in its sadness/mess much like I do in my shame/severe need to cry profusely out of situations I cannot control. FML.

"Why is that even allowed online? There's nudity!"

"Don't worry Jiles, I'm sure it will be taken down as soon as the moderators see nudity. But hey, you'll probably garner some more fans?"

Only Cory would know how to comfort me in the most embarrassing thing that has ever happened to me. I decide I'll speak nothing of it. I am so desperate for Cory to forget this whole laughing matter. But I wonder what he thought of my bare rump!

Her song ends and the men toss her over cat calls and whistles galore. They all think Cory is the luckiest guy in the room, but it seems like Cory feels the complete opposite.

"So, what are you doing out?" he asks.

"I just finished my last shift on 94X, so I figured I'd give myself a pat on the back. And by back I mean my liver. And by pat I mean a DWI."

Cory laughs as his little lady sits down alongside him, and it's only now do I see how much make up she truly has on. Well, little body, big tits.

"Hi!" she exclaims and sticks her hand out. "I'm Vicki! I'm sorry we met on such bad circumstances."

Her composure seems too elevated to be natural. I immediately assume she's on coke. Her smile is annoyingly perky, her teeth are too white to be natural, and her skin is too flawless to be realistic. It must be nice to be so put together. But is it worth losing an hour's sleep to do this? No, never.

"Oh you met me when I was drunk and fell asleep in my lawn chair that I knocked over?" I burst her bubble with some serious sarcasm.

She looks lost but Cory laughs at my obvious joke from a night he clearly remembers.

"You fell asleep out there?"

"Yes sir, it was the most interesting way I'd ever woken up. The sad part is, that wasn't the worst thing that happened to me that day. I tried to rub one out an hour earlier, and I thought I was super wet and horny. Turns out it was just my period that came a day earlier, you should have seen the look on my face when I saw my fingers!"

I'm sure that was too much for them, but I'm just aching to say all the wrong things in front of this girl. Instead of being horrified, Cory spits out his drink into a fine mist and puts his head down in his folded arms. He attempts to calm himself all the while writhing with laughter. I can't help but admire the shakes of his body caused not by my sexual prowess, but because of my trademark humor and unfortunately true story.

"So Jiles, are you going to do a song?" she asks, attempting to clear up the fact that she was left out of our inside joke. Territorial, she is, and not at all down to laugh at my hilarious misfortune.

"Oh man no!" I scrunch my face in at this hideous notion, swallowing more beer as I nod my head like a yoyo. Side to side that is.

"Why not? I thought you were a performer."

I survey her with bitter resentment, she's trying to put me on the spot so I'll feel like a jackass. I know this isn't her intention, but its the only result that will come of me being on stage for a reason other than telling jokes.

"Yeah come on Jiles, go on up!" Cory nudges my arm. I think the fact that he even touched me pissed her off, because she clears her throat as loudly as she can while putting her own hand on his arm.

"Honey, don't punch her," she smiles even if her tone is irked.

"Ya know what, I have been working on something. I'll give it a go," I say, getting up and going to sign up with the poor dude who has to register people.

"Hey are you Jiles Perry?" the sign up sheet man asks. I notice he's got a bandana on.

"Yeah, thanks for remembering my sorry ass face. Can I borrow that real quick mate?" I point to his bandana.

I quickly wrap the bandana around my cranium where the little twist is at the top. I wonder if anyone gets the joke yet, since I'm in an Ottawa jersey.

"Next up, our very own stand up comedian, Jiles Perry! Singing *California Love,* the announcer cheers with as much enthusiasm as I wish Cory had for me. His date is clapping even harder, what a fucking show off. She's trying too hard to kiss my ass so that Cory will think she plays wells with others. The truth? I bet she's called me a hairy dyke in the three minutes I've been gone.

"Austin Texas Love," I sing before the song starts up.

The beat comes on and everyone starts laughing immediately when they figure out I'm going to do a parody of this very classic rap song.

"Let me welcome everyone to the Lone Star State
Except Austin is the only part that is great
This city is just light years above the rest
Ladies so free it's legal to show off the breast
Hipsters lurking on every single beat
Underage vomit all over 6th street
Senators on a mission for them drunk ass teens
Getting popular votes by any means
If you get hungry no need for a car
Yummy food trucks up and down South Lamar
Mack on *Mmmpanadas* with high quality flour
But get out of here before rush hour
Traffic so hectic they had to make a tollway
Your city is da bomb if your city making pay
Take 130 going 85 all the way
To Dallas...or somewhere else that's gay

If you like live music we got venues galore
*Southby*, *ACL* and oh so much more
Celebs chilling at all of these fests
Wake up in the morning with 94X
Ben and Brodie, that fat dude is the best
In Austin we wearing *Toms* cause we eco friendly
Banned plastic bags, biodegradable enemies

They call it Silicon Valley of the South
Brainiacs with knowledge coming out they' mouth
Underage girls attending *UTA*
Chill on Guadalupe and scope the free T&A
Run on the trails of Zilker Park
But get your ass home before dark
If you get get raped you're screwed
Cause Rick Perry tells vaginas what to do
Wendy Davis should filibust a cap up his ass
She's gonna be *Batman* of bat city!"

[A/N:See the real video at Vanessaloveshockey.com]

Everyone is laughing throughout my song of improvised
lyrics that include hipsters, the bag ban, the governor's
vagina plan, and the surrounding cities that wish they were
Austin. In fact, a couple of guys come up to me and start
dancing just to dance when I say 'Shake it baby, shake it. I
cannot shake it cause I'm Canadian.' I'm grinning a legit
smile and remembering that while having big boobs might
be nice, having a sense of humour will bring the men flying
faster. I see this disdain in her eyes, wondering why she
herself didn't have men running up to sing along with her.
Cory is impressed with my choice, smiling earnestly but
when I see her whisper something to him, he drops his
expression immediately.

My song ends and I get a far more impressive
clap-athon than lady *Spice Girl*. I take the bandana off and
hand it back to the gent.

"Give it up for Jiles Perry, who you can see perform
soon at the *Paramount Theatre* for her first *HBO* taping!" I
hear behind me. I'm so incredibly high on my new ego, if I
weren't at least a tad heavy I would have floated away. "You
can also see her boogie down on *YouTube*!"

"SHH!" I say to the announcer but it's clearly too late. You know that ego I had a second ago? Yeah, it's gone.

"Jiles that was awesome!" Cory pats me on the back when I sit down. I see he's quite impressed, Vicki is not.

"Interesting song choice," Vicki stops trying to play nice, taking a sip of her girly ass cocktail. I can't help but notice her nails are bedazzled. They are all so perfectly shaped and polished, making her hands look like a model when she holds the stem of her drink. I wonder if she vajazzles her pussy too.

"Yeah, that was cool as hell, thanks for the encouragement," I taunt her, knowing full well that the only reason people are looking at my table now is because I'm sitting at it.

Cory attempts not to look at me in the eyes even though his happiness for me is pure: he knows I need recovery and optimism post divorce. Every spoonful of encouragement is a step in the right direction, but the *Spice Girl* took the spoon out of Cory's hand and shoved it up her ass before I could even see it.

"So Jiles, do you still talk to your ex?" she asks.

Both Cory and I stare silently off into space, shocked that she'd bring such an insensitive topic up. I decide I will be the bigger person, I won't allow her low brow attempts to be the successful woman at the table get to me.

"No, not at all. He's a little bitch."

"You should have Cory set you up with one of the

players. I bet you'd love someone as handsome and strong as my man," she gushes, holding his face in her hand and giving him a theatrical kiss, one that he doesn't seem to enjoy.

"That's okay, I'm not in any rush to get laid," I purse my lips as I watch her continue to force smooches on Cory. His cheek is a fluorescent red from her department store lipstick and he tries gently to push her off without using brute force.

"Lets go home," she says loudly. Was that supposed to be seductive?

"I'm having fun," Cory denies her, taking another sip of his drink as he looks over at me. He sees my enjoyment at what an ass she's making of herself and I can tell that he'd be willing to spend a day in my shoes just to have my perspective of this hilarious show.

"Well I want to go home, and I bet that a lot of men would like to go home with me too," she pouts, folding her arms and looking away. I guess I shouldn't be so surprised at what a baby card she is playing, but Cory clearly isn't amused.

"I can meet up with you later if you want," Cory ignores her heeding, but he's cut short when a squeal becomes so loud it punctures both of our ear drums.

"The girls are here!" Vicki jumps up.

I watch her boobs bounce up and down as she leaps from the table and goes running to....OH NO...more ice girls! They reunion jump into a pillow fight kind of hug fest like they didn't just see each other earlier at work. And what do you know? They're all sporting their uniforms.

Before they can even look back and Vicki has to explain why I'm at their table, I am out my seat and scattered like a *Mostel 9* roach when the lights go on. They leave the lamp on for you so the roaches scramble hours before you get there. I stand near the side of the bar and hover since there are no empty seats.

"Hey Jiles, can I have your autograph?" a gentleman asks me that I'm standing behind. He swings his chair around and hands me a coaster and a pen. "That was an awesome parody. Do you want my seat?"

"No thanks, I sit on my ass too much anyway," I say while forging my own shitty signature. It used to be more professional when I though this was the coolest thing ever. This will probably wind up in a junk drawer with a vibrator or a flesh light.

"Who are those girls were you were with?" he asks me, looking at my former table to see it's now covered with shiny haired women all in the same get up. And of course poor Cory, who seems to be the one that wants to leave now.

"Not my friends I can promise you that. You'd think they were rejects from the *Kick Ass* movie in those get ups. Who else goes around wearing a cheerleader outfit all fucking day?"

Within a few minutes of making small talk with the fan sitting before me, a few other people have come up to me to ask for a photo and inquire about my show. I tell a few jokes and a few of them even ask me to do my infamous rap song that helped me win *Funniest Person*. I get over my minute of shyness and bust right into it.

"You ran over my yard gnome, and now you're getting sued!

If you think gnomes aren't alive, you are mother fucking rude!

He was my best friend and his name was Nick, time to pay the price you man-slaughtering dick

You wanna start a beef? Go eat a burger bitch!

The court dates next month, you're gonna make me rich

Don't say you weren't warned , if you do you got nerve

So show your ass in court, cause you just got served!"

At this point, I've totally stolen the thunder of whoever is performing at the moment.

"What the fuck?" one of the ice girls interrupts their group performance of a *Pussy Cat Dolls* song when they hear mad applause and see the circle of men around me as I do my bit.

My interested audience erupts into a volcano of tears: tears rimmed with the taste of saltiness to go along with the tequila shots they're holding. They're around me like we're watching a guy in Miami break dance with neon kicks and gold teeth in an empty downtown street. It's probably empty because the hobos scared everyone away, but even the hobos are afraid of this wild pack of laughter.

When the commotion dies down, they spread out backward and everyone else in the bar takes view to the fact that it's me getting all of the attention. Even Cory is looking in my direction. Needless to say, the ice girls are furious. Oh no, I ruined their performance!

A few of them march up to me to see what all of the brouhaha is.

"Telling jokes during our song? Real mature," a taller girl states, black curly hair and more black eye make up than she needs. I see the sad fact of sincerity in her eyes and how she's profusely pissed that someone like me could steal her thunder when compared to her, I'm dressed like a lady of Saudi Arabia.

"I was just doing what these guys asked me to do."

"Well next time learn some manners, we were trying to do a song. After all, this is karaoke night. Not open mic night. By the way, I can shake my ass better than you on that little webcam!" she laughs at me, turning around and purposefully shaking her rump to get the guys that were enjoying my company to go chasing her. God, what showmanship!

I brush off whatever level of snobbery was just presented to me and go back to having a good time with my new mates. I pass out some extra tickets I have to the taping to all of the cool people that decided not to ditch me to follow her butt.

The ice girls do their routine again and I continue ignoring them, still opting to stand so I don't have to sit at their table. Cory gets up and comes over to me mid song.

"I hope they haven't been too rude to you," he whispers. I admire the fact that he's wiped away her lipstick, now his own natural pink hues are showing. His skin is so flawless without make up of any kind- now that's a real beauty. I stare at his eye lashes and wonder how he got them to be so long.

"Uh, yeah well, they can't do any worse than what they've already done, ya know?" I shrug it off.

"Still, it's lame. I feel kind of embarrassed being here with them. I don't see why they can't change into regular clothes. I wouldn't go around in my Partisans gear just to get attention. That's a hypothetical situation set in Ottawa, because no one would care if I walked around in Assassins gear here."

We both laugh at his unfortunately true commentary, our happiness cut off when their song is over and Vicki comes storming over, her hubris wounded in only a way that neglectful parents can make a kid feel. Too bad she's an adult.

"Why weren't you watching?" she pouts yet again, her glossy bubblegum lips looking as duck face as ever, glaring at him with more ice than found in a rink.

"I just wanted to make sure Jiles was okay," he tilts his head, looking back at me and secretly wishing she'd just shut up.

"Jiles isn't your girlfriend, I am!" she complains. "Let's go home, now," she grabs his arm and surprisingly has enough strength to drag him away.

"Bye Jiles," he calls out. His pleading eyes are highlighted with a tint of desperation. This is because I know deep down behind her sexy body, he'd rather be with me. Sex lasts for minutes, but true hometown companionship abroad is priceless. After all, you can pay for a hooker.

I decide to change bars and go somewhere a little quieter with no divas performing or prancing around in their Sunday best. This is only one place: *Pluckers*. Those girls won't go anywhere in which calories, beers, or sports are served. Ironic seeing how they work for a sports team. The bartender puts on the Partisans game halfway through (it's being played on pacific time as they are in southern California) and I enjoy the quiet rest of my night with a late dinner, beer, and my favourite men. These guys would never get dragged away by bitchy women.

Over the next few days I don't run into Cory because, as the stalker that I am, I know he is on the road in the east coast until his Vancouver Moose game at home. The night he arrives, I do however, overhear him bringing home Vicki. It still horrifies me how fast some ice girl can sink her teeth into a guy. Cory's been here barely a few weeks, what the hell. I'm sure it's just the jealously talking, but for now I will continue to trash these girls as I see fit. Tonight I'm heading down to the *Paramount Theatre* where I will be filming my taping. I'm going to rehearse while they tape it and I'll re-watch it afterwards to see how I like it. It's going to be weird rehearsing jokes to virtually no one. A few folks are coming but no one I know. Mainly just the venue employee's friends. I prefer it that way, the less people that know me, the better.

"Don't forget about tomorrow," Cory texts me. He happened to slip his number in a very old school style, on a sheet of paper under my door. It was the sexiest way I've ever gotten a guy's number. What he means about tomorrow is that I'm going to that hockey game that I promised him I'd go to. I'm still not happy about it, its got my body in a total tizzy! Will I burst out crying when the ice girls come out? Stay tuned!

# CHAPTER 14

I'm sweating my ass off in preparation of this Moose/Asses game. I don't know if I'll be able to shake my postpartum depression of this faulty marriage aftermath. After all, I'll have to watch the bitch on the jumbo tron. I guess I could just keep my head down, but still, knowing she is there will make it hard.

I enter the arena with such chills to be in a place I once loved, a place I vowed I'd probably never come to again. Security searches me, probably for good reason. I'd expect me to have a gun too. Thanks to Cory and his swanky connections, I strut myself all the way down to the glass, taking a seat behind the bench. I hope he will sit in front of me for his off ice time, because I will need him to smile at me to help me get through this night. Of course, I would be happy to be behind the Moose too. I need these home reminders as the way to remind myself that this isn't the end of the world. This too shall pass.

I am wearing a Moose jersey that I ordered with overnight shipping. I still have to make it known that I do not want to be here or help support an organization in anyway that supports home wreckers for employees. Moose don't have that shit, neither do my Partisans. I completely understand that the team has nothing to do with it, but she hath forever tain-teth my feelings for the Austin Asses.

I decide to go buy a craft beer from one of the many booze stops, because I think we all know I will need booze to calm my nerves. Back in the day when I was a broke mofo,

I would go to the "Responsible Driver" table and fill out the info form to get a coupon for a free small soda. While I am a responsible driver, I couldn't afford the beer anyway. I should have gone to every table to get more coupons, but alas I'm a lazy jew. I would however, scope out some tables for free promo goodies. I have a lot of random things from my years of attending games: foam goalie masks, player figurines, towels, magazines, and best yet, a failed marriage!

"Ladies and gentleman," I hear over the entire arena as folks start to gather in their seats. "We've got a wonderful announcement to make for the fans of the visiting team. The Trenton Triangle Arena is proud to offer our very own *Tim Horton's*! We've even got *Tim Bits*!"

Wow. Just wow. For those of you that aren't familiar, *Tim Horton's* is the chain-iest of chains in Canada, offering coffee and donuts, *Tim Bits* being the donut holes. Did they really think all of the Vancouver fans were gonna lose their shit because they have something we can get on every street 362 days of the year? Those last 3 being the days spent here, of course.

For Americans, let's put it this way. Say *McDonald's* was only in the USA. If a group of Austin fans went up to Canada to watch a hockey game and they were all "We've got *McD's*! We've even got *McNuggets*!", wouldn't you be like, uh....so?

Thought so.

The buzzer sounds as I stare at the cold empty ice, wishing I could be back in Ottawa where my safety zone is, where this may have never happened to me because that girl's job wouldn't have existed. The players from both teams come on out as do the excited onlookers who stand by the glass with homemade signs and take pics of the players whizzing by. I see all of the popular names of both teams since I stand in the centre, opting not to take pictures. I'm not excited to be here, remember?

I see Cory come shooting passed me as he goes around in his warm up, passing shots to some other left and right wingers. He shoots a puck at me as he flies by again. I watch as they take practice shots on their goaltender, who manages to stop most of them. Where is that capability during the real fucking game?

Koenig comes by again and decides to press his back up against the glass to watch for his next opportunity to practice a shot. While he waits, he turns to face me.

"You okay?" he mouths.

I give him my 'I don't know' shrug, and a sloppy bottom lip smile. He tosses a puck over the glass and I catch it. Before he takes off again, he winks at me. I wish these winks were for the classic, 'Hey good looking!' and not this, 'I'm sorry your husband left you cause you're not hot' wink.

I decide to sit back down with my prized puck and read the game booklet I was given. Of course, there is a photo of the ice girls and there she is. That smug cunt with her brown curly hair. Her tiny eye brows and too much fucking make up. Big fishy lips and even bigger tits. Her waist is disgustingly small, and yet everyone thinks she's the hottest ass of them all. I close my book shut and enjoy more of my beer. And some *Tim Bits*. Because yeah, I wanted some. Don't judge me! I haven't been home in a while.

T he game is great as far as sports are concerned because I get to see some top talent from both teams, and it's tied 2-2 by the time the 3rd period ends. Cory does sit in front of me and looks back every once in a while, and even more so, when he's leaving for intermissions he looks at me and smiles. I don't understand why he's trying so hard to get me to be happy.

Unfortunately, the moment I dreaded came. The cheerleading squad came out and did their thang, getting guys to focus in on them over all else. I looked away and couldn't help but look around at the club suites. I just knew that bastard was there, drooling over her the way he secretly did when we'd go to games together.

Another unfortunate thing happened that I won't go into too much detail: during the intermission someone decided to play my ass dance with a blurry box over my butt on the JUMBO-TRON! Seriously?! Who is the dick that decided this was appropriate? Just what I needed, another reason to fucking hate the Asses.

The game ended up going into a shoot out and Ass-assins won, which was a total surprise to me. When I got to the main floor to exit, my phone buzzed immediately.

"Where are you?" Cory asks. Gotta say, I like that he only gave me one ticket. In my dreams, it was his way of saying, 'This isn't your date with another guy!"

"I'm on the first floor."

"Come on down to the locker room. Just ask an usher and show him the badge I gave you. He'll escort you down."

I find an usher and show him my so called credentials and sure enough, he's taking me down a route I've never been before. I'm living a fucking Canadian's dream! As I go downstairs, I get to see the media hounding locker rooms as the men are still shirtless, probably scrubbing the sweat off their ball sacks. I lean my head against the wall and watch as the players slowly come trickling down, going in different directions. I suppose it's in everybody's best interest that opposing teams don't intermingle in case a scuffle ensues.

I can't help but gush when I see the Moose start coming out, players I totally worship. Bob Baker, their star goaltender, smiles at me in my shock and awe, other players secretly giggling at my enthusiasm. Full on Reginald mode going on here. Suddenly I see someone walking in my direction and it looks as if he's coming to talk to me.

"Excuse me, are you Jiles Perry?" a black haired gentlemen with a face as hunky as David Boreanaz asks.

"Holy shit, you're Kal Kargman and you know who I am?" I don't even hold back, my voice in shrill freak out mode.

"Yeah, I saw you in Vancouver last month, you were hilarious! I read about you online that night and saw you lived here. I was hoping you'd be doing a show while I was in town."

"Oh my gosh, I'm so honoured sir!"

"Don't be nervous, I'm just as excited to meet you!" he tries to calm me down.

Let me fill you in here. Kal Kargman has this sexy, crisp tanned like skin even if he's from Ontario. His jaw line is totally strong, and his features are as defined as I assume his cock is too. Plus he's got these gorgeous lips that just ooze, 'I'm a damn good kisser!'

"My team doesn't fly out until tomorrow noonish, do you have any plans tonight?"

"Uh, I'm not sure to be honest. I came down here because of Cory," I say. Good timing too, as Cory is coming out all dressed up in his suit. Did I mention they all wear suits post game? Something I've never understood but hey, they all look damn good so no complaints here!

"Jiles, I see you're feeling better," he chirps in before realizing who I'm talking to.

"Oh hey Kal. We used to be on the Manitoba farm team back in the day," he tells me, apparently familiar with my new fan. "Jiles is my neighbor."

"Wow, you get to live next door to her? I'm jealous of you dude."

"You know her?" Cory asks.

"Yeah, I saw her show in Vancouver a few months ago. This woman is fucking hilarious, and she knows her hockey."

I'm melting, really. Since when do people I'm a fan of even know I exist as anything more than a stupid, speechless fan? I'm smiling so wide and for some reason, I feel a hint of jealousy in Cory's tone. He is slightly taken by shock that Kal is into me.

"I haven't see Jiles perform yet."

"You haven't huh? Good," Kal looks back and winks at me. I like where this is going. "So, are you free?" he asks me again.

"Cory, did you want to post game party with us?" I ask him.

"Yeah, let's go get a drink," he decides. I didn't think he'd say yes. I really am feeling a hint of jealousy.

# CHAPTER 15

Kal, Cory and I sit at a high circular table at *J Blacks*, throwing back whiskey like it's water. I slow my roll but these boys obviously deserve their fun. They probably sweat out all of the toxins of alcohol just walking to the team bus. Me? Eh.

"So Jiles, how'd you wind up in Austin, you're from Ottawa right?" Kal asks me, sitting dangerously close.

"I wanted to go to college in the States, I decided I wanted to get a taste of the world and why not start with the next country? Besides, Austin seems like NYC but for po' folks."

"How'd you become a Moose fan?" he says, admiring the jersey with his name on it, ironically.

"Actually I'm not too big of a fan, I just hate the Ass-assins and so I root against them."

"She has good reason," Cory defends me.

"Why's that?" Kal asks, his hand propping up his uber sexy chin as he apparently admires my face. His intensity is shooting across the table faster than his goal tonight.

"I..uh..."

"Want me to tell him?" Cory expresses his sympathies to me. I nod yes.

"She's getting divorced because her ex husband left her for one of those ice girls."

"Oh wow, I'm so sorry to hear that Jiles." Kal moves closer and takes my hand. "He sounds like a fucking moron. Who is dumb enough to leave you?" he rubs my hand even, a glimmer in his eyes that make it clear he's into me. I'm glad I decide to tweeze my eyebrows tonight!

"Thank you. How long have you two known each other?"

"Kal and I were on the same team back in 2006 when we got to the championship. We shared a dorm on the road. And this guy, he's a total fucking slob!" Cory laughs. I wonder if this is an attempt to get me uninterested.

"Ah come on, I wasn't that bad!" Kal defends himself, not at all bothered by the comment.

"Yeah he was, he would leave used condom wrappers around the room as a practical joke!"

"What?" I snicker, clearly Cory doesn't know I think gross shit is funny.

Cory gives Kal a look, but Kal looks back with a, 'WTF are you doing man, I'm trying to get laid!' face. He looks back at me with the same macho smile I saw him with as he approached me.

"Practical jokes, eh? I like it! Comedy is my game, after all! Too bad there are no playoffs for me."

"There are a few things you could score," Kal flirts with

another wink.

"OKAY! It's getting late, I think we should call it a night," Cory slams his hand on the table, clearly irked at Kal's obvious advances.

"You tired already bro?" Kal works his defensive skills both on and off the ice.

"Yeah, I got more ice time than usual. And you have a flight to catch right? Don't you have a time to be back at the hotel, like, now?"

"No man, as long as I stumble in before they leave I'm good."

It's clear Kal doesn't sense Cory's tone, or maybe he does and he just doesn't want to be cock blocked.

"It's a shame I have to share a room with another player, I'm rooming with Wiggins."

"Oh that's too bad. I live by myself, obviously. Our building is really upscale and it's right here in downtown too."

"Oh yeah? Why don't you show me your place?" Kal asks. My vagina is already wet. Hoooo yeah.


**A**fter we pay for our drinks (Okay, Kal paid for them because he's obviously trying to woo me), we go outside and hail a cab. I sit in the centre and from Cory's body language, he's obviously mad at me.

"Are you okay, Cory?" I ask him on our ride to defeat the awkward silence.

"Yeah, why wouldn't I be?"

"Thank you so much for the game tonight. It was so nice to get back in there. It was hard at times though. She was in the booklet, and I avoided watching their stupid dance numbers."

Cory looks into my eyes with a genuine grin, his sincere hope for me to be happy sitting in there.

"I'm glad. You can't let one woman ruin your whole hockey experience. You were born to be a fan, and we can't lose real fans like you in a town where the team clearly needs them."

Cory bends his back straight to see behind me, finding that Kal has his hand on the small of my back. The cab comes to a stop and we get out. The elevator is equally as quiet. I debate suggesting a three way, which I would absolutely be down for.

"This was broken when I came back from my tour, so we were walking up 14 flights. I was so hung over I threw up in the stairwell, the walk was so nauseating!" I admit to Kal.

"That was you?!" Cory laughs, thanking me for once again murdering the silence.

"That was some trademark Jiles Perry vomit you saw in the hallway. I feel bad for leaving it there, but they can hire someone to clean that shit up since they clearly can't hire someone to fix the elevator."

We step out on our floor and Cory gives us this stare, this one that looks like he's just pleading for Kal to go away. Or maybe it's just because I know that's what he's thinking.

"Well, it was nice to see you again Kal. We'll have to meet up next time you guys are in town."

"Yeah man, great to see you. And thanks for bringing this girl along with you," he puts his hand around my waist.

"Yeah, so, uh, goodnight guys," Cory quickly spits out and goes in. He slams his door as his final way of telling us not to fuck.

I am totally flattered to see that Cory feels something for me period, but the fact is, he is dating an ice girl and has never shown any interest in me. So why am I going to sit here and pass the ass of a hunk for a guy who shows nothing for me?

As soon as we're inside, Kal grabs my hand and walks me to my sofa. He pulls me down to sit beside him and throws those hot lips on mine. Those lips? I am indeed right. Will my second fuck ever be from a Vancouver Moose?

Yes, yes it is.

As we get our clothes off, Kal asks me where my room is and carries me like it's nothing but another hockey stick, mainly because much like the stick I have no boobs. He kisses me everywhere I hoped he would, eating me out for a few minutes. I only worry slightly about my less than clean shaven vag, but decide in the end guys usually don't give a fuck in the heat of the moment. He's so good at this I'm trembling, even more so because I know Cory can hear me moaning. I hope he's jealous but at the same token, I'm worried this will affect how he sees me.

Before I can worry anymore, Kal tosses me on top of his body, sliding me down onto his dick with one quick motion. As soon as he feels he's inside, the defensemen uses his brute strength to thrust me faster than my lame ass *Toyota* ever could. I'm moaning moans I never thought I would have a reason to exhale, pleasures I never knew I could feel.

"Damn Jiles you feel so fucking good," he moans somewhere in the middle of this unforgettable lay for me. I quickly realize how much I regret not setting up a camera in here, that way I'd have an actual video of me and my name being said to play loudly for Cory. But he may recognize Kal's voice and find out what's up about my pathetic attempt to look cool. Only these stupid things would race through my mind when the hottest guy on the Vancouver Moose is in my pants.

I hear something being thrown in Cory's room. I guess that means he can definitely hear me and is pissed, or he tossed his clothes off to jerk it listening to me. The ultimate flattery of tonight? Having a hockey player masturbating to the sound of me moaning while I'm being fucked by an equally hot hockey player. Tonight is most definitely a Canadian's dream.

# CHAPTER 16

I wake up at 10am thanks to the ole alarm and see a text from Ben. We're meeting up today for the weekend o' fun. Kal caught a cab back to the player's hotel room last night, that fancy smanshy *W hotel*. I walked him downstairs and kissed him as he got into the cab. Even with my big bucks these days, I don't think I could stay somewhere like that. I'm more of a *Super 8/Days Inn* kind of girl. I mean fuck, *Holiday Inn* is my idea of upscale. $100 for a night is silly no matter how much money you make. He gave me his number and told me he couldn't wait to see me again, saying he wished I would relocate to Vancouver. As I went back into my place, I considered asking Cory why he seemed pissed when he made it clear I was just his friend. But instead I went to sleep.

I spruced myself up a bit more than usual this morning, mainly because I'm still reeling in the highlights of my incredable (I'm trying to do this french, go along!) orgasms last night. Tres magnifique, that Kargman's bed skills! My hair is straightened and I tossed on some light make up too. I put on some casual flip flops to go along with my overall theme of weekend on the water. Shorts and a tank top; I don't prefer skirts, ever. That's because I have a bad habit of sitting down and spreading them wide. Manners, class, me? Nope.

My mother calls before I'm about to step out. This scares me since we have a code that no calls before noon unless it is an emergency. "What up, ma?" I answer.

"Jiles! Why is there a video of your butt online?! Your brother showed it to me this morning!"

"It was a joke ma.... yes it was intentional......no I was not being held captive and forced against my will....look I gotta go okay....well I'm sorry you think my comedy is gross....okay I gotta go...bye."

That call was actually 10 minutes. I hardly got a word in while she yelled at me.

I close the door to my apartment and find that Cory is once again leaving at the same time. He's toting a suitcase and in his pressed navy suit. A slight argyle pattern makes me laugh a tad but I'm not one to insult people's clothing choices.

"Away weekend?" I ask him.

"Yeah, we've got some games on the west coast. You?"

"I'm going to New Braunfels with my friend, floating the river and then a concert. Should be a good weekend," I say nonchalantly. I know Cory is going to say something about what transpired last night.

We both hop onto the elevator that came quickly; it came faster than me last night. Cory lets me on first, such a mannerly young lad. I hold the door as he steps on.

"So, how was he?"

I cannot help but laugh at this very forward remark, a comment normally made by someone like, oh I don't know, me.

"Good, I guess. I don't know to be honest. He was the first person that's been with me, since..."

My pathetic truth seems to touch Cory because he suddenly drops all disdain in his eyes, now looking at me like a deer in headlights. He gasps a little, putting his hand on my shoulder.

"Oh wow, I had no idea Jiles. Hey, I'm happy for you, it's good to break out of your shell. Did you give your husband your virginity?"

"Yeah, I was a sucker back then. I guess I'm on the right path now. I never wanted to be someone that fucked every guy in sight, but last night was the first time someone made me feel wanted since I met my ex, so it was nice. I feel 25% woman again."

I don't know if I should smile or feel like a loser that he now feels bad from trying to cock block me from my second lay ever.

"I'm happy for you, I am. You're an awesome girl Jiles, someone will want you again, I promise."

The doors open and I realize I've left my phone on my coffee table.

"Shit, I gotta go back up, I left my phone on my table."

"I need to get going, I hate being last on the flight. Have a fun weekend hun," he departs but not before giving me a kiss on the cheek. I look up in the midst of this and see his long eye lashes covering what may be a sign of attraction. His eyelashes are more feminine that mine.

As I go back up, I wonder why he felt the need to kiss me. I'm not complaining, I just want to know if this is going in the direction I so badly wanted it to.

**B**en and I sit on our joint inner tube as we float along the Comal River in San Marcos. It's a nice tradition a lot of people do in the Austin/San Anton' area. There aren't too many folks out since it is technically fall, but luckily for us Texans it's still in the temperatures that would make anyone take a dive into the water for a few moments to cool down. In Ottawa it's probably cresting into the 40's, snow making its way steady and slowly into the atmosphere. This is why I love Texas.

Ben says it's his treat for filling in for Brodie. He bought the inner tube, drove us down, and even bought a case of crafty beers to sit in the middle. The cool thing about this joint inner tube? It's comes with a spot in the middle to hold ice and booze. Oh how well this inner tube knows us. The only thing we'd let come in the middle of our friendship is beer.

After we go flying through the first shoot, where a stupid ass tween gets knocked over by our device, we're smooth sailing with not too bad of a crowd.

"Why do kids stand right there at the shoot exit and then give us the stink eye when we knock them over? They know where they're standing," Ben bitches and I wholeheartedly agree.

"I enjoy the challenge of knocking 'em over," I declare as I slide deep into my inner tube, splashing my feet into the cool running river. The surface is totally visible, barely about

7 inches deep at some points. Hell, there are parts when I'm scraping my ass along the surface.

"How was the Asses game?"

"Well, despite the part where they showed me dancing with my ass out on the jumbo-tron!" I punch him hard on the shoulder. "It went good, really good. Cory actually had me come down to the players exit and I got to see some of the Moose. Even better, one of them knew me from my show in Vancouver. He used to play with Cory so we all went out for drinks."

"THREE WAY!" Ben laughs.

"No no, more like a, two way," I proclaim with bravado.

"Jiles Perry, are you telling me you had sex with a second person in your life?"

"I sure did, and damn, he was good! This guy was a babe man, I cannot believe he knew who the fuck I was. More importantly, I cannot believe that guy thought I was cute!"

"Aw come on Jiles, you're adorable."

"Nah. But this guy, Kal Kargman, hot damn. He's the kind of guy I'd use one of my cheesy pick up lines on, like, "Hey baby, you should come home with me because in the morning, I make a dayymmmmnn good breakfast!""

Ben laughs at my bit, looking over and giving my body the once over. Maybe he can tell I'm radiating from getting laid. "So did you cook him breakfast?"

"No, he left afterward, had to get back to the team hotel. You know how it is, poor guys are whipped on their schedules. Strangely enough, I think ole Cory was jealous."

"What makes you say that?"

"He was angry about Kal making obvious passes at me. Slammed his door when we got home. I think he heard us fucking too."

"Good. That's what he gets for that parade of ice girls he's bringing home. It's only fair."

"I suppose. It feels weird to know I've had sex with two people now."

"And I was always hoping I'd be your number two," Ben jokes, splashing some water at me. "Remember when we used to come here in college after exams?"

"Yeah. I'm glad we never did that with *Nissan Altima*. It would totally ruin this moment. He always said he was above this because it seemed like something only frat boys would do."

"We all have a little frat in us," Ben admits, holding up his shitty pilsner to the sun. A few rays sneak through the bottle and give me an odd view of the sun's vast array. I'm blinded for a moment. When my sight comes back, I think I see someone I recognize. "Oh shit!"

"What?" I ask.

"Please tell me I'm seeing things. I think I see *Nissan* over there."

I look passed Ben's body a few feet down and spot a back of the head that looks terribly familiar, caramel brown hair a little too grown out for your modern day businessman. But I don't need to confirm it's him when I see who he is with. Another tube floats along side with a woman whose body looks like the kind that men would leave a wife over. It's them.

"Un fucking believable. What is he doing here?!" I whisper. The panic in my system is at an all time high, it feels like I've stalked him and now I'm being caught in the act.

"Wow, is that the ice girl? Va va voom!"

"Ben! Quick, hide me."

"With what? I have nothing, unless you want me to sit on top of you."

"Shit, we're going to go past them any moment now!" I panic. In my moment of great haste, I decide there's only one option. I push myself up and throw myself into the water, thankful it's deep enough again that I didn't slam my face into a rock. I grab onto the rope tied along the side and drag our joint tube while I swim with my head under the water. I go up for air and hear Ben immediately.

"Keep going, they can still see you," he says low enough that I can hear but they can't. I plunge myself into the cool flowing stream and continue to push us as fast as I can. I do this until I can't hold my breathe anymore.

"Am I good?" I manage to say in the midst of trying to catch a much needed breath.

"Yeah, you're good! I didn't think you could pull my fat ass that quick," Ben admires between sips of booze.

"God, what the fuck was that for?" I bitch, getting back into my spot. I reach for my drink immediately and start chugging away.

"Shit happens," is all he consoles me with. He starts replenishing his body with sunscreen, since after all, he is a ginger. "Get my back?" he asks, handing me the bottle. I rub the creamy white substance and watch as it disintegrates into his skin, admiring his sweaty pores and the area where his tattoo once sat, lasered off from his body. No one needs a *Limp Bizkit* tattoo. His skin is terribly hot and I wonder how he is comfortable at all. Right now, doing this task is mundane but it detracts my panicking heart from the chaos I just ensued.

An hour has passed and we're halfway through. I've gone through all of my beers and refuse to touch any of his.

*"Oh oh oh oh oh, you [don't wanna get sued] go, oh oh oh oh oh oh,"* I sing with only the enthusiasm that a depressed drunk could have after being left by their spouse. Oh wait, that is me.

"Try a more upbeat tune. Like, *"if it keeps [don't wanna get sued] going to break,"* he sings.

"It's because your fat ass was on it," I toss in.

"Because you're hurting, I'll accept it. I know you didn't mean it," he justifies, a tad drunk himself.

"This is a disaster. I came out here to have fun man. That dick just ruins everything for me."

"That's not true! You're having fun with me and after this we get to go see the mother fucking *Toadies*!" he shouts with enthusiasm like we're a bunch of drunk college kids.

"You sound like a frat boy. And I don't want *Hyundai* to be right about anything."

"You know why he says that? Because frat boys know how to have a good fucking time! And he clearly doesn't. It took a young slut to drag his ass out here because he was too stupid to know what a good time was."

"Touche Benny."

I lean my head back on the hot rubber material of my tube. I let the beer I've downed continue to relax my anxious heart as we flow further down the Comal.

Instead of enjoying the view of the water, I stare at him instead. His slight red stubble is coming back in even if he just shaved yesterday. A small goatee established with the connector between his sideburns sit in perfect length, but he refuses to have a full on beard and mustache. I think it's because he knows that's just too much ginger. His hair is at average rock star style, messy and sticking up.

Unfortunately for Ben, this isn't him trying to be cool, this is him just being lazy. He wears what I call douche shades, plastic neon sunglasses that he got for free at some promotional event. When he isn't wearing them on his face, he still wears them on his face. And by that I mean he manages to keep them on his body just by putting the ends around his neck. AKA his neck is big enough to keep them in place. He's never dropped them once. That's scary!

I think about the colour of his eyes and wish I could see them for a minute but I don't think staring into someone's eyes after I've asked them to take their sunglasses off is ever not creepy. Even if he is my good friend, I wouldn't want to risk creeping him out that way. I look back to the water and hope we're zooming fast enough to stay away from that bastard.

Two hours later we're standing at the front of the pit for *The Toadies* annual show, *Dia De Las Toadies. The Toadies* are a fantabulous Texas band that had their hay day in the 90's, but god do we still love them or what? Ben and I are pretty damn drunk at this point. We chowed down at some little German place before taking a cab over to the outdoor show. Because of his connections, we get to come right up to the front. He still has a beer in his hand but I've had my fill. We both happen to have the same favourite *Toadies* song, so when it comes on we both sing along at the top of our lungs like good ole drunks would. It's in this moment that I'm feeling more alive than ever, enjoying company with someone who is probably the last person I can trust anymore. It's come down to this.

So when I drunkenly toss my arm around his shoulder, he looks at me with a catch I've never seen before. Then he leans down and gives me a quick kiss on the lips. Maybe it was the drinks, maybe it was the sincere chemistry, but after the show I find myself in his half of the suite making out on his bed.

"What are we doing?" I ask the second he pulls away.

"Having fun sex with an awesome chick."

"I don't know man, is this a bad idea? I don't want to ruin our friendship. You're my only friend."

"How would we ruin it Jiles? I just want to experience you in my life in a new way."

Because I'm drunk and depressed, I let it happen. In no time Ben has our clothes on the floor and he's slamming his hardness into my wetness. He's so big the bed shakes more than I thought a bed could, and I'm so thankful this is happening at a hotel and not my place. It's too dark for us to look into each other's eyes, which I'm also thankful for. I don't think either of us need to see each other in that light. He flips it on post sex so he can find his way around the room.

"So, how was I?" Ben asks after he lays back down from tossing off the condom and washing his hands. I had no idea he was a cleanly kind of guy. Most folks just toss a used condom to the floor in a hotel and to hell with their hands. No wait, that's me! My mistake.

"Both you and Kal were way better than *Fiat*. And uh, I hope things won't be awkward between us."

"They won't. I like you, kid."

Ben reaches over and turns off the lamp, then puts his arm around me. I'm totally surprised at this move.

"Let me tell you a funny story about this one time I came to see *The Toadies*. I had driven down here after a late remote with a pack of chicks at like 2 in the morning, and we're all so wa..."

Ben is snoring away and I laugh at his odd ball behaviour. He's the only guy I know that can fall asleep mid sentence, even snoring in the same minute.

# CHAPTER 17

After a quick lunch with more beer, we're heading back to town. We don't talk much about what happened last night other than the part where I reiterate how he fell asleep mid sentence, and I crack jokes about how badly he shook the bed. Ben doesn't get offended by any joke, which is probably one of my favourite things about him. There aren't enough people in this world who can let insults just roll off their back fat the way Ben White can.

"Let's go do a drive by and bust someone," Ben says as we re-enter Austin city limits. I wonder if he means a gang bust of some sort until we're down a familiar path, parking in front of Brodie's place.

Brodie opens the door in her work out gear, sweating and clearly smelling.

"So, you're too sick to work but you can work out?" Ben questions.

"Come on in," she rolls her eyes and we step inside. Brodie's house is clean as can be except for her dog, Grey, who is running around and eating shit left and right. Broken window blinds hang in the kitchen waiting to be replaced, as is the window in her car where Grey has eaten the peel around the frame.

"Be honest, you weren't sick," Ben asks again.

"Okay here's the deal guys, I was sick. But only for a

day or two," the Aussie admits, leading us to take a seat on her sofa. She sits on her ottoman across from us, giving us both eye interaction. "After that, I just figured, I missed three days, why not miss the last of them. You'd do it too. I tried to plan a last minute flight to see my family but damn are round trip flights to Australia expense!"

She has no regrets, clearly living her life the way any person dreams. Brodie is gorgeous: she's rocking a brunette pixie cut and got the sexy accent to top it off. In my opinion, she's the hottest chick in Austin. Fuck those ice girls.

"Jiles, you did a good job this week," she smiles at me, patting my knee.

"Jiles' husband left her for an ice girl," Ben spills my beans.

"What?" Brodie's mouth hangs and I see her eyes dilate at this juicy scoop. "Which one? *Sporty*?"

"An ICE girl," I clarify to her. "I think everyone mishears that as *Spice Girl*. Maybe it's because being left by a *Spice Girl* is more realistic than some no name ice girl."

"Oh hun, I'm so sorry! Did this jackass take advantage of you?" she immediately questions Ben's motives as to why he called me in, flashing her glare in his direction.

"No no, he's just the only guy left in town I trust."

"What a cock sucker. Ford, not you Ben," she quickly says to him. "You don't need him, you're going to be a comedian at the top of the chain and he's just some boring finance guy. What's an ice girl anyway?"

"Someone who cheerleads for the Austin Assassins," Ben tells her.

"Oh yeah? Well you're on the up and up, you will find someone far better than him."

"Well actually, I would give anything to go on a date with my neighbor, but he doesn't see me as anything more than a dude."

"He thinks you're gay?"

"No, I mean he's not attracted to me at all. Although he acted a little funny on Friday when he saw me with another guy. But he is seeing an ice girl himself. There's no way that dude would want me over those figure skaters gone bad."

"Is he worth getting a little make over?"

"Nooo...yeah, maybe. I don't want to have to change myself for someone's admiration."

"I value and completely understand your opinion, but we all need a little make over once and a while. How about you come over after the show tomorrow and I'll take you to get a bit of a freshing up."

"You mean waxing my vag? Because I haven't done that in like 6 months."

"I noticed," Ben points out with no shame in admitting our deeds.

"EW BEN! I knew you'd take advantage of her, you ass!" she smacks him playfully on the head.

"It's okay, I was desperate," I chime in.

"You and me both!" Ben smiles at me with a sweetness behind his eyes that means it's no insult. I don't know if Ben has feelings for me or not, but I'd say if we could get over the hurdle of fucking up our friendship, he'd be the perfect soul mate. Well, perfect if he liked hockey too.

Because I'm not filling in for Brodie, I spend the rest of Sunday night up late catching up with the games I've missed on my DVR. I even watched a few Ass-Assins games just to see how Cory did. Tomorrow he's playing in Colorado and then he'll be home. I wonder if that means a late flight tomorrow or early the next morning.

I managed to fall asleep on my sofa at some point, waking up to see my TV asking me if I'd like to delete the Partisans recording. The way they lost last night? Hell yes I would. It's noon already and I see a text on my phone.

"Yo, are we still on for a glammy makeover?"

It's Brodie, I didn't know she had my digits. I assume Ben gave her my number.

"Sure, what time?" I text back.

"I'm gonna go work out, after that? Or maybe you'd like to come work out with me? I can bring a guest for free," she responds. Me, work out? Ha. Well...

"I guess I could start living better, new life, new me," I text back.

Brodie gives me the address to her gym and tells me to bring certain work out items. The funny thing is, because I've never worked out a day in my life, I have none of that shit other than average tennis shoes. I decide a pair of sweat pants and an old Partisans hoodie will do the trick.

Wrong. I look like a fucking fat girl at a sleep over when I get to this cross fit class. Brodie looks hot as eff in her tight work out pants and a bra type gym piece. The only thing we have in common is the old head band.

"This is cross fit. It's intense, but you'll get the hang of it. I promise you'll feel amazing afterwards. I come here three times a week."

An hour later, I'm ready to strangle Brodie. This work out feels more like Hitler took over the class and made us poor jews move around until we couldn't see straight. I forgot to throw on deodorant so I stink worse than I normally do, which is all the time. I nearly fell on my face twice trying to do poses I didn't even know were possible. How did anyone come up with these workouts? Brodie laughs at me when she sees the faces I'm making, those of pure agony and desperation for this to be over. If this is small peanuts compared to labor, why the fuck would anyone have a baby? I can hardly get over taking a mediocre painful dump.

"Class dismissed," Hitler says and I let myself fall to the floor.

"Jiles, it wasn't that bad," Brodie kicks me lightly on the side, motioning for me to get up.

"Dude, are you fucking kidding me? I thought we were gonna do a treadmill. This was bullshit," I continue to lay on the ground, hoping my sweat will trickle down and off of me.

"Having a good body is a bitch, but so's life," she instructs me. She has her hands poised perfectly on her hips, those that are as well defined as my neighbor. Maybe they deserve each other. God knows I don't care about my health like these two do.

"And so are you for taking me here," I say without thinking. Brodie is a no nonsense chick, so instead of giving me a lecture, she kicks my ribs and walks off. I roll over in agony, grabbing my ribs like Tyson just threw me a swift jab.

When the pain subsides and I've caught my breath, I hobble into the showers where Brodie convinces me to share a shower with her.

"Are you a lesbian?" I ask her as I shyly step in to our dual shower. I'm glad I told her beforehand that I hadn't shaved my pubes, otherwise I'd have some 'splaining to do.

"No, of course not, but we're all ladies here and I'm not shy. I didn't think you were either. Besides, I need to see what I'm working with here."

"Working with? Are we fucking later?" I laugh, beginning to loofa my chest.

"Jiles, I think it's clear the best way to get passed your divorce is to change up a lot about your life. Granted you're uber successful and probably outearning me now, it's good to get fit. Mentally and physically. Your husband left you for a better looking woman."

"Hey!"

"Oh come on, we're not fooling anyone! We both know those ice girls have a better body and they're all pretty. It doesn't mean they are better people per se, it just means they are more pleasing to the eye. I'm not saying we need to become them, but the race is on. Don't you want that prick to see you again and feel like a jackass for leaving you?"

"I didn't even think I'd see him again."

"This is Austin, not Houston. You will. We run in the same circles, same bars. You know you'll see him again. And if not to put him in his place, do it for yourself. The more in shape you are, I promise you'll have more self confidence. It radiates. From what I can see, you're in decent shape, but you need to tone up. So maybe you can just work out with me at the gym until you're cross fit ready. Otherwise, after this we will get you a little hair change up and some make up, shall we?"

"Aye aye, captain," I salute her with one hand while I've got the loofa up my ass crack.

B rodie takes me into some salon with a name I don't care to remember because it looks too hard for me to remember. Le Chateau De Hair or some shit like that. Yeah, I think that was it.

"What are we doing?" the stylist says, a guy who reminds me of the server Cory and I had on our first shindig.

"She just needs to freshen up, I can't say I know what's best for her. Maybe you can help me out here. This Jiles is a lost cause," she pouts, standing behind me with her perfectly "coiffed" hair. Coif, what a word.

"Hmm, how about we give her some layers and bangs," he suggests in his ultra femme voice, femme-ier than mine even. His hair too is "coiffed."

"Lay her and bang, that's all I heard," I shrug. A piece of my trade mark humour floats off everywhere I go and finds a way to ruin any legit sentence.

While the guy is cutting my hair, Brodie sits along side and drinks the complimentary herbal tea offered to guests.

"I like that you're here solo too. I don't mean relationship wise, I just meant that we're both foreigners without any family. It's a little gloomy sometimes huh?"

"It does get a little hard. I spent every Thanksgiving with my ex's family. I spent a lot of Christmas' with them too. It's going to be weird going it alone now."

"How about we spend those together. I will start a refugee for all displaced citizens who are forced to be in the holiday season alone."

"Why don't you go home more often?" I ask.

"I love Australia, it's just that the ride is an absolute bitch. And it's just so much money. I don't have a problem with paying for it when I plan it out in advance, but it's just a little cringing to see how much I blow for a week."

"I guess I don't really have an excuse, Ottawa isn't far."

"You should spend more time at home, Jiles. You've got the means to do anything you'd like. I miss my family so much, I would kill to be in your position to go see them any time I wanted."

Brodie is just infusing so much good advice on me, it feels like she's my mother. After my cut, she takes me to another joint where they show me what 'hues' go with my skin and what colours compliment me. I think it's all just a guess, but if they say they're pros, I'll believe it. When all is said and done, I look in the mirror and cannot even believe it. Brodie has turned me from a pumpkin to a carriage. No wait, I mean a woman!

She's so excited for me that she manages to drag me to dinner with some of her friends. I've met a few of them on occasion but I don't know them too well. They're a bit more hmm..should I say outgoing? In the looks department and chatting it up with the social scene that is. Most people have told me that I have a lot of balls to do stand up, which to me is far easier than trying to look good. We swap stories and laugh it up, drinking to the point that it's almost midnight and none of us have realized it.

"Shit, it's my bed time!" Brodie jumps up despite the drink in her hand, making it fly up and spill over her arm. She throws down what she thinks she owes on the table and comes over to me. Because we rode together from the gym, she takes me with her even though I am game for more hours on the town. But Brodie knows best!

I finally enter my elevator, getting up to my floor completely forgetting how 'dolled up' I am. And as usual, Cory is in the hall with his suitcase, reaching into his black messenger bag for his home keys. He gives me a double take, and that's when I realize Brodie is right. I'm feeling so high by something I could have done by myself so easily had I just cared enough to try.

"Wow, Jiles! You look amazing," he smiles at me, spinning around even to watch me go to my door on the left of his.

"Thanks, you just get in?"

"Yeah, we flew in right after the game."

"How was it?"

"Eh, we lost, but I got two assists."

"Good job," I say sincerely as I unlock my door. I cannot help but stare at him as I do so. I want him to take me all in, drink up every ounce of me that I hope he secretly wants to caress.

"If you don't mind me asking, were you on a date? Last time I checked, Vancouver wasn't playing here again until April," he grins, still eyeing me with disbelief.

"Not at all. My girlfriend took me to get a haircut and some make up shit, then I went to dinner with her entourage. It was my first girls night on the town," I say with finger quotations.

"I'm surprised you didn't get a lot of numbers," he says with a calmness that denotes maybe he's relieved I didn't.

"No, but I did take a shower with a super hot woman, good night!" I end for a hilarious closing line as I shut the door behind myself. I set my purchases down and lean back on my door, breathing a sigh of something new. I think it's called satisfaction, and fuck did that feel good.

# CHAPTER 18

I'm sound asleep until I hear banging on my door. It sounds so urgent that I leap out of bed and go charging forward. I open up to see Cory with sheer panic in his eyes.

"What the hell Cory?"

"I need your help! There's no time to explain!" he commands like a captain, taking my hand and marches toward my patio. He slides open the door and drags me on out.

"What's out here?"

Before I can even look at him for his response, he grips my hand and we go flying off, up and away.

"CORY! What the fuck is going on?!" I panic at our out of this world move. I look below my moose jammies and see that we've skyrocketed many miles away from planet Earth, as I can now make out the continents and the swirls of the oceans. The air flaps hard against us but I do not feel pain. I look at Cory as he holds my hand tight, his hair has grown a bit longer and he has some stubble going on. He's so gingerly today it's hurting my eyes when the star's light reflects on the ends.

"The King of the Gingers has requested our services, the Queen of Nice has been kidnapped and we must rescue her!"

"The Queen of Nice? Rosie O'Donnell?"

"No! Rosie was the Queen in the 90's, but now she's all angry with the world or maybe just Trump."

"So who are we saving?"

Cory says nothing as I see we are shooting forward to a planet half the size of our home. It's a pale peach color and what do you know? It has freckles. "This is Gingeria. My home planet."

Cory uses his muscle to force our momentum downward, slowing us down even as we come into view of a red castle. A moat and large cement fence keep trespassers out, I take notice, before we land on the castle's grounds. The grass is red, as you could have guessed. The plush feeling of the dewy red grass lightly soaks the feet of my jammies. Every step is like walking on a moist, warm cloth.

Cory knocks on a very archaic looking wooden door, an elegant brown shade with no flaws despite its obvious age. Instantly it creeps open. We're greeted by...oh no...Carrot Top.

"Well hello," he smiles widely at us, showcasing his large choppers. "The King has been expecting you two," he coos almost in a song and starts to skip his way down the main hallway. He wears a red suit, which is ridiculous. Not because it's red, but because no one would ever take Carrot Top seriously.

I take a quick peek at our surroundings as we follow, noticing paintings of red headed kings and queens posing for oil paintings. The floor is made of cement, which seems trashy for a castle. I've seen houses like that in Louisiana. Does this mean Louisiana is a step ahead of the rest in terms of royalty? God I hope not!

Carrot Top assumes a steadfast position outside of an even larger set of doors. He holds his head up high and shouts, "YOUR MAJESTY!"

His simple words cause the door to open, slamming outward into the wall. Carrot Top has to take a quick sprint to avoid being smashed into the wall by the automatic door. Cory takes my hand and we continue into a room clearly meant for the king. This room has similar floors and not much else beyond a grandeur wooden desk in the centre. A large leather recliner sits before it facing out the massive window. I see some red hair and a crown from this man's head. He's watching a red headed jester playing a guitar. This jester is quite tall himself, dancing around in a green and white, tight one piece with bells on the ends of his hat. It takes me but a second to realize this is Joshua Homme from *Queens of the Stone Age*! That's one hot red head alright. Maybe even hotter than Cory.

"Oh what you've done to me? I don't know," he sings in a high note while flicking his fingers against a glittery, red guitar.

He stops playing as soon as he notices our viewership. The king snaps his finger and Homme disappears.

The chair spins in our direction, revealing the King of Gingeria. And of course what ginger could it be but the one and only, Conan O'Brien. And that crown? Yeah, it's a *Burger King* crown. He's eating some fries too. He also dons a black cape that covers whatever else he may be wearing. He grins at us, eyeing my pajamas like I'm the crazy one in this dream.

"You bought along your own jester I see, Koenig?"

"Yes sir."

"Well, I'm glad you both made it. I need you both to save the Queen of Nice! I need her to repopulate Gingeria from the massive case of sun that killed off almost half of our population. Gingeria's fate is in your hands!"

"What should we do?"

"Take the Gingeriamobile and stop the evil brunettes from destroying her! And kidnap Mila Kunis while you're at it!"

"Does she cause harm to our country sir?"

"Uh....yes. She will cause harm, to my ability to hold out!" he starts laughing maniacally and slams his hand on the desk. Dust goes flying in every direction, some in his face that causes him to cough.

"We really need a maid around here. Now seriously, hurry! Appear, mobile!" he shouts at the empty space beside his desk, pointing forcefully with his index finger. He's scrunched his face up like he's trying to control telekinesis with the muscles in his face. "I said, appear mobile!"

Nothing happens. He sighs heavily and looks in our direction, shaking his massive head in shame. "Nothing works around here. What is this? The 94X studio? Carrot Top, bring in the *E.T.* Bicycle!"

Carrot Top rushes in with the bicycle from the movie. Cory jumps on and waits for me to figure out how I will get on.

"Get in the basket, Jiles," Cory instructs me. Ah geez.

I manage to lift myself without straining my vag against the basket while I climb aboard. This is more ridiculous than the entire dream! I do manage to fit snugly within, crossing my legs as I prepare for my front row view of wherever the hell we are off to.

Cory starts peddling forward, lifting us up into the sky as a hole appears in the ceiling for our escape. Within seconds, we are passing by the moon, our silhouette as trademark infringing as you would expect.

We land on another planet, one with an illusion of a brown glowing ball. Quickly as we lower to the surface, we pass through their atmosphere down into an odd lair of some sort that you would find in a lame 90's video game. The floor is a sleek black plastic, which I must say, looks hell of a lot better than that ragged castle. Before us is a large tube with a woman trapped inside. She looks familiar...

"You dragged me out of bed to save the ice girl that destroyed my marriage?!" I shout at Cory, fully furious that the Queen of Nice just so happens to be the cunt of destruction.

"Jiles, you must put your spite behind you! Just save her! The clock is ticking, she's about to explode!"

"5....4...." I overhear around us, a large clock on the wall showing her that her death is near. Good.

"Be the bigger person Jiles! Be a hero!"

"3....2..."

"Cory, mmmm."

"That feels so good!"

"What?" I look back to see Cory is in a full fledged make out session with Mila Kunis. What the hell?

"I...."

"Oh yeah Cory!" she continues to moan when he grabs ahold of her bum.

I open my eyes. I'm in my room and I hear moaning coming from behind the wall. Ah geez. Morning sex? Well, at least they woke me up before I had to watch Katie the Marriage Killer blow to smithereens. What a dream, eh?

# CHAPTER 19

It's night time and I'm doing exactly what you think I'm doing. No! I'm not drinking. I'm watching a Vancouver Moose game. I decided I wanted to see more of Kal since he's the only guy that's touched old 'puss in dread locks' for quite some time.

"And there goes Kargman starting a brawl with the Calgary rookie defensemen Shale," the TV announcer states the obvious. I watch as Kal tosses his gloves off and gives the rookie this cute smile and wink, like he's saying, 'show me what you got boy!' Hey, that's almost the look he gave me when got me totally naked. Man, I gotta get my ass to Vancouver. This is hot!

Kal doesn't really try to hurt him, just a bit of brotherly horseplay to show the kid not to mess with the veterans. Kal is taken into the penalty box where he's applauded by his fan base, still holding a smirk as strongly as his muscles are implanted throughout his body. Dear god. I'm so horny.

So I do the ole one two and whip my moose jammie zipper down, getting ready for a fun time jerking off to a man in the penalty box. I sure wish I were a penalty box. Come on in Kal, you can do your 2 minutes in here just like ole *Daewoo Lanos*. That's a car if you're unfamiliar.

The second my finger brushes against my joystick, I hear my name being called. Is that Kal coming across the TV?! I hear it again and realize it's coming from behind my head.

"Uh, yeah?"

"I'm having some of the guys over. Why don't you stop on by at 8pm?" he speaks from his room. It's slightly muffled, but for the most part I understand it all.

"Oh, sure."

Phew. For a second I thought he was gonna say he knew I was jerking it. Meet some Austin Asses huh? This should be interesting.

I go in my jammies and knock on the door after having spent 30 minutes contemplating if I should be early or late. Isn't it lame to be the first person at a party? Like you were too eager and had nothing else to do? I'm sure Cory knew I was doing nothing, especially considering he killed my zam-boner earlier.

"Hey, glad you made it," Cory applauses me as if I were too lazy to walk a few feet.

"Made it? You say this as if I wasn't sitting on the other side of the wall."

"Why didn't you come by earlier then?"

"I had better things to do, like, decide what to wear."

"And you chose your pajamas?"

"Yes, yes I did." Deny it till you die, my friend.

"Hey guys," Cory turns to a few folks on the sofas,

faces that I know but I'm not exactly sure who is what position. "This is my neighbor Jiles, she's a stand up comedian from Ottawa."

They give me a loud Bronx cheer because they are all Canadians themselves, and boy howdy do we love to find our fellow brothers and sisters out and about.

"Ottawa huh? You a Partisans fan?" Mason Murrows asks me on the patio after he finishes off another brewski.

"I'm a die-hard. You should have have seen the look on my face when I found Cory living next door. It was a literal dream come true."

"Lucky dog. The people next door still have no idea who I am. I bet they think I play peewee hockey."

"Fuck them, less people hounding you for tickets! How do you like being down in Texas?"

"It's got its privileges, but overall I find it a difficult contrast. I grew up playing hockey on a pond, and now I'm living somewhere that almost never sees snow. I've been here for 3 years now and I've seen it snow once, barely a few centimeters. You should have seen how these fuckers reacted, like it was the Apocalypse. I think that's the best day of the year to find your fellow Canadians, we are the only people on the road when the city shuts down."

"Yeah buddy, we're some brave mofos," I high five him.

"So, what's your problem with the ice girls?" he asks. Is my hatred that well known?

"I just think they bring a lame element to the game. I mean, were there ice girls on the ponds when you learned as a kid? It's a sport that people spend their whole lives dedicated to, and then you get to the big leagues and they're all, 'Hey! Let's add some folks who do nothing but dance to entertain you when you should be admiring the people who have made their dreams come true.' To me, it's plain ole stupid. It brings hockey down a notch in terms of honour."

"I completely get what you are saying. I think they're a waste of money myself, but if it brings in more fans, I'm all for it," he explains. Damn him and his good reasoning.

"Do they hit on you?"

"No, I'm married."

"Didn't stop that cunt Katie."

"What do you mean?" he raises an eyebrow, one that has a scar from a hit a few years ago. He attempts a bushy brow look but I can always see the scars on a player's face.

"My ex husband left me for her."

"Why didn't you just tell me that's why you hated them? That makes so much more sense."

He gives me a hug with an extra pat on the back. His strength is very duly noted. It feels amazing to be in these men's arms, even if it's just a sympathetic hug.

"EEE!" I hear a squeal from the inside. Mason and I look back to see the girls entering, once again in a group, and still in their outfits. I'm starting to think they really do get paid like shit. It seems as if they cannot afford a wardrobe.

"Do you know why they never change their clothes?" I ask Murrows with a scoff.

"No idea, I guess they like the notoriety. They're probably more recognized than the team."

"Every time I see them in their outfits as a pack, I think they're going to bust out into a musical number. This ain't *West Side Story*!"

"Well, the more the merrier, eh? Let's go inside."

I decide to follow him against my better judgment. I just want to be comfortable around them since it's clear they will be a part of my life for as long as Cory is a part of it. What a fucked up trade off. You can see this hot guy you love IF you are willing to put up with people you hate! So basically every wife understand this if they hate their in-laws.

"Jiles, do you ever change your clothes?" one of the girls snaps at me while I'm pouring myself a beer. She's the girl that approached me at the bar that one night.

"Funny, I was wondering the same thing about you."

"What you're wearing is not exactly street friendly."

"Oh really? I had no idea wearing booty shorts and a bra type shirt was."

"Don't be so bitter Jiles. Katie is the one that stole your husband, not us. With your attitude it's no surprise either."

"Ya know what. FUCK YOU! You don't fucking know

anything about me. And it's clear you don't have a goddamn sense of humour if all you do is judge me for wearing some comfortable pajamas at my home! My life was fine until Austin had to incorporate your stupid ass gig so please, tell me I'm an asshole for covering up my body and trying to make people laugh. I'd sure as hell rather be funny than a fucking slut!"

Everyone is looking at me now. Murrows is about to laugh his ass off, his face holding it together but I see the strain in his cheeks to keep quiet. I decide I need to get the hell out of here, which is exactly what I do.

I lean on my door and breathe deeply. I know I've ruined my chances with Cory even more. But what does it matter when I never had a chance with him in the first place?

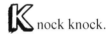nock knock.

Hmm..is it Murrows to console me or Cory to yell at me for my behaviour? I open up without taking a peek out. Low and behold. It's one of the ice girls. She's the only black girl on the team, which frightens me a little. I'm about to get my ass kicked huh? Her skin is a light creamy shade and she's a little bit bigger than the other girls. I don't mean in weight, but her bone structure. Of course, her body is still better than mine.

"I need to talk to you honey," she comes right out, walking passed me and taking a seat. Ballsy, this one is.

"Uh, welcome?" I take a seat along side her.

"Jiles, you can't hate the entire squad because of one

incident."

"You're kidding right. It's not just about the divorce. You guys wear that shit everywhere, stop being so obsessed for attention."

"Hey it's a fun outfit okay! I like to wear this because it's comfortable. Just like you like to wear your moose thing."

"Are you telling me having a perpetual wedgie is as comfortable as pajamas?"

"Jiles, enough with the jokes," she rolls her eyes. "Let's get real here. You hate me and you don't even know me."

"I don't hate you."

"Well you just told off Cassie and basically insulted her as well as the rest of us. You don't know us just as much as we don't know you."

"What I know about you guys, I don't like," I clearly state. My tone is so reasonable, it's almost like we aren't in the beginning of an argument.

"Girl please, you don't know a lot about me. Some of the girls are in college and they are just doing this for the extra money that their scholarships didn't cover."

"No way. They have the brain cells to go to college AND get a scholarship?"

She bops me on the back of the head. My head bounces forward like a balloon. Fuck she's strong! "No more jokes Jiles. I'm Canon by the way."

"Canon?"

"Yes ma'am, I shoot out like-"

"AH! I don't want to hear your cum skills, please."

"I'm just saying you need to give us a chance. I don't appreciate having enemies when I've done nothing wrong. I've worked really hard and now I'm just having fun with this job. I won't do this forever, I've got big plans in my future."

"Like what? *Hooters*?"

Canon moans quietly in frustration. Clearly she's had it with my *Chandler Bing* attitude. But who doesn't love a good sarcastic person that's sex starved! I notice her hair is perfectly straightened and almost as long as my own. She sports a thick coat of black mascara that draw her eyelashes out as long as a spider. Her lips are full and curvy, in perfect line with the rest of her deemed 'rocking body.' I tell you this because of what I'm about to find out.

"Jiles, I'm gonna be famous one day. I'm gonna be all over the internet, on TV giving out interviews, maybe even on stage."

"Doing what? Porn."

"NO! I'm going to write a tell all book so I can prove that men are just as good of cheerleaders as women. Jiles, look at me," she takes her hands on the sides of my face and pulls me toward her. "I'm a man."

My eyes grow almost Reginald size but I keep my body

form. She's bullshitting me. Or is it he.

"WHAT?"

"Sssh! I've never told anyone this, ever. I had a sex change five years ago. No one knows and I'm going to keep it that way until I'm too old to do this job."

"Are you fucking kidding me?! Are you honestly telling me that a man looks better than me?!"

She laughs, looking over my body in the process. "Yes, I am."

"No way. That's insane. God, I'm ugly."

"Girl, you aren't ugly. You're just lazy and spiteful."

"Wait a minute....Canon...Canon...Oh my god! Were you on this year's Christmas *Maury* show?"

"Yes, I was," she blows on her nails with bravado. "I'm impressed, most people don't know that."

"I knew you looked familiar. It was the "Man or Woman," episode! How have you not been caught then?"

"I made sure we were out at a Christmas party when it aired."

"You clever dog."

"So Jiles, do you still hate me? I just told you something that I've never breathed to a soul since I moved here."

"I don't hate you. I don't hate anyone. I'm just still

hurting. And having you guys all around my life isn't easy," I dutifully try to let her down easy. I'm really not trying to be an asshole to RuPaul here.

"I know it's not honey," she/he puts her/his arm around me and gives me a light tug closer. "Let's be friends okay?"

"Fine. But only because I love the *Maury* show."

"Let's go back in there."

"No way!"

"Will you do it if I wear your moose pajamas?"

"What will I wear?"

Ⓒanon and I go back into Cory's house. Canon is sincerely stretching out my jammies in the boob area, and me? I'm deflating her ice girls outfit. Holy bananas this thing is uncomfortable. Way to much skin on display. She didn't even give me a chance to shave my legs, so here I am like a gorilla.

"Ladies, Jiles has something she'd like to say," Canon announces to the room. Everyone stops to look at us. Surprisingly, no one has said anything about us changing outfits.

"This outfit sucks," I snarl and Canon pinches my ear. "Ow! Ow! Okay, okay!" She lets me go and I get ready to play nice. There are a million voices in my head asking me why on Gingeria I'm about to try and play nice with these girls. It takes everything in me to say these next words. It feels like my first open mic night all over again.

"I'm sorry I insulted you ladies. I know I shouldn't blame you all for what happened. I just don't know how to handle having you beautiful ladies everywhere I go, a constant reminder of what I lack and how it lead me to losing my husband. I apologize."

"AWWW!" the girls all whimper in unison. They run up to me and hug me. I'm dying in a sea of perfumes ranging from *Jen Aniston* to *Faith Hill*, and even a *Bieber*. I realize Canon is wearing the *Bieber*. What's worse? That Canon is wearing Justin Bieber cologne? Or that I happen to know what that snot nosed punk's perfume smells like? I don't care if he's a Canadian. I do not support!

"Katie is a total bitch, she thinks she's better than all of us!"

"For real girlfriend! Why don't you let us give you a makeover?"

"You look super cute in our outfit, we should get her one don't you girls think?"

They're all talking over each other and I just want to breathe again so I say the only thing I know that will get them to scoot away. "I have to shit."

They step back in unison like it's a dance routine. It probably is. To honour my lie, I head to Cory's bathroom. Before I get to the door, he steps up and blocks me from entering.

"Hey, I'm proud of you Jiles. You're not too far gone after all."

"What can I say? I'm no good at being a dick. That's why I am the one that got left."

"I hope I never meet this guy, or that ice girl. You're a great person, truly," he smirks to one side and gives me a hug. He even peppers in a kiss on the cheek. I wonder how much ass kissing I would have to do for the ice girls before Cory redirects that kiss a little lower south. "They aren't so bad, eh? Nice girls."

"Yeah, girls alright," I snicker to myself. I like this Canon. I can tell I'm gonna have a lot of fun with her.

# CHAPTER 20

"Don't tell me you're going to bail out of the Partisans game!" Cory asks when he knocks on my door at noon and sees me in my pajamas.

"Uh...no, I wasn't."

"I figured with them in town you would have been out stalking their hotel room."

"I would, but I know I can just hit you for that information. My stalking days are over sir."

"Well I got you a pair of seats behind the enemy bench."

"Holy shit, thank you so much dude!" I smile earnestly and hug him.

"I know you can afford them yourself, but I figured you still need some coaxing into coming to the games. Remember, tonight you need to forget all about your douche ex and those girls. Tonight, it's about hockey. It's about our home, our team, our tradition. Mother fucking Partisans baby," he slips into the sexiest smile I've ever seen, holy crap. I'm so horny and wet that I may slip when I step back.

"Are you telling me you want Ottawa to win tonight?"

"Of course, but I'll try my best not to make it that obvious. I won't fuck up on purpose, I just hope I can rely on good ole Ass-assins to suck."

"You're the greatest."

"And hey, don't bring a date," he winks at me before returning to his pad.

I'm melting deep down when I turn around with my prized seats. Row C, seats 3 and 4, also known as 'behind the bench' seats. All I can imagine is that I'll oogle the Partisans sitting before me, studying their neck hair and anything else I can get a peek at. I jump up with only a move that can be drawn for an *Archie* comic in celebration. Ya know, the one where *Archie* clasps his feet together while making a diamond shape between his legs, all miraculously still in the air? Yeah, that one. Wahoo!

"Ben, what are you doing tonight?" I text him in hopes I'm not interrupting his afternoon nap. I forgot how crucial that nap is now that I'm back to having absolutely nothing to do.

"I've got a secret underground poker game. What's up?"

"Aw shit, hockey boy gave me some bench seats so I thought you would like to join me," I text back.

"Ask Brodie, I bet she'd be down. She's just as horny as you."

I wonder if this is a good combo at a hockey game: two foreigners sitting behind a bench of some gorgeous men, and decide this sounds like an absolute blast.

"Brodie, you wanna come with me for three hours so we can stare at some athletes behind a glass like rotisserie chicken?"

She calls me back immediately with questions galore, like what to wear since it will be cold, if any of the players are single, and oh yeah, what event is it. By 5pm she's parked in my garage and we cab it to the arena, the mighty Trenton Triangle.

We enjoy our club status on the tickets and pay for overpriced drinks, which I'm convinced is the only thing keeping the Asses organization afloat. I'm a tad embarrassed that Brodie isn't at all sporting anything Partisans on her garb because it will make her look like an Asses fan, which is pretty humiliating. She's in some fancy black tights that she swears are warm, sexy navy boots, and some weird blouse that doesn't qualify as a blouse if you ask me. She tops it off with a fitting sweater featuring ruffles on the ends.

Brodie is so in the know about what's cool. Or that's what I tell myself about her outfits. Her brunette hair is edgy as ever and her make up compliments her outfit. I happen to love her look because she's always walking around with confidence and I wish I could walk into this cloud and take some of that with me. Too bad it's her cotton candy and it dissolves as soon as I try to bite into it.

And me? I'm in my extra small Partisans' Carlson jersey and blue jeans. But I did bother to toss on some make up. And by that I mean Brodie put it on me. She tossed foundation and it hit me in the face; she has good aim.

"These are the guys? Wow!" Brodie exclaims in her thick Aussie accent when the men come rolling, or should I say skating on out and park their keisters in front of us. She eyes them all with a glow and excitement that I wish I could feel. I lost all of that when *Mercedes* stole my hockey pride.

As the game wears on, I spend much of the first period explaining to Brodie what's going on when calls and penalties are assessed. She at least gets the hint not to cheer when the Asses score.

"Oh that's Cory," I say when he skates passed us. He looks over at us and smiles even though it's clear they never want players to interact with the fans during the game.

"WOW! I cannot believe it, I honestly expected him to be average at best but man alive! Can I come live with you? I wouldn't mind listening to that guy get laid every day."

"It's not every day."

"It's more than you!"

"I know, you're right. To think, I boned the terribly inflated version of that guy."

"You mean Ben's weight?"

"And ego!"

The first period winds down with a power play but my Partisans fail to capitalize. Everyone is happy but me, Brodie, and the few other Partisans fans here. It's always nice to see fellow Canadians, or just fellow hockey enthusiasts who happen to support Ottawa, probably Canada's least favourite team.

During the second period intermission, more people fill in the seats on the lower bowl and I can only imagine they are people from the top that scouted empty seats and are proclaiming them now. Unfortunately, this ushers in a large group of yuppies and general southern trash. It's my theory that they only come here because they cannot afford football games so this is their outlet to acting like a fucker at a sporting event. And it's even more unfortunate that they've decided to heckle the player on the closest end of the bench. I listen to then chant at poor Neil and then at MacArthur when he is in that spot. I assume these idiots only do this because they don't know anyone on the team so they wait to see a back and read that name. They are lucky Wiercioch or Khabibulan aren't sitting there.

It's grinding my gears more and more to hear this so I start flailing shit back but I doubt they hear me. I look over at them and see this idiot in a flat billed hat, the douche-iest look in the book. He also happens to be in a cast for his foot. I think about how the idiot broke his foot, probably in a stupid attempt to copy something he saw on *Jackass*, because he is indeed a jackass. His posse of 'tards are a few other guys who probably just all turned of age because they hold crap light like it's a goddamn glass of whiskey. And as you all know, I think popular light beers are the worst. There's also two girls with them, one is drunk and the other looks bored out of her mind. The drunk one is a blonde princess type, an ice girl in the making.

"Oh geez, it's the ice girls," Brodie says at first sight of them doing a stupid dance number on the second level of seating.

They wear their dumb revealing outfits and shake pompoms like maracas, moving their butts to whatever this stupid rap song is that's apparently cool. But then I see Canon with a huge smile on her face and she's having so much fun. It's hard for me to hate on my new friend. After all, the fact that she used to have meatballs and a bread stick makes me love her to death. I cannot wait to see the look on those girl's faces when she fucks them up with some truth.

She's pulling the best prank ever on the ice girls, which I completely support.

"Cheerleading at a hockey game is a joke, and so are these morons here heckling the Partisans. I didn't pay for this seat so I could spend the game more distracted at what these fuckers are saying to people I love."

"I thought you said these tickets were free."

"I paid for them out of love for the sport Brodie!"

The third period rolls around and it's not looking good. Partisans have only scored once and the goddamn Asses have 3 goals. I'm listening to these fuckers heckle the guys over and over as if they have no need to breathe. I'm seething but I'm doing my best to keep it under wraps. Brodie is also annoyed, not that she cares what they are saying, but that they are loud and it's distracting. For a seat so good, you want to be invested in the game, not at the commentary of some jack off.

"Can I ask you something?" Brodie faces her entire body toward me. How dare she ignore the game!

"Yes, this is a bad night for Ottawa. I promise they are normally good," I keep my eyes fixed on the ice.

"Do you have feelings for Ben?"

This simple sentence pulls me out of this disaster of a game and I face her in return.

"I don't think so. Why?"

"Why did you have sex with him then?"

"We were both drunk, and I was upset. We ran into my ex and his new girl. Why?"

"Uh, it's just that...Ben lied. He had no poker game tonight. He text me immediately and asked me not to say no to you because he didn't want to show up." She grimaces, and the fact that this is over Ben means it's serious. Ben never gets empathy from anyone. "He is afraid that he has feelings for you and thinks it would ruin your friendship. I guess he feels distancing himself from you will make it go away."

"I never thought Ben would be such a pussy over drunk sex," I cannot help but admit. I really am such a man sometimes.

"Hey, I was surprised too. But I'm proud of him for finally having real emotions. And it's nice to see how much he truly values you as a friend above all."

"You're right, I'm flattered. Well, tell him he has nothing to fear. I can think of thousands of ways to end any idea he may have of him liking me. I'm talking shitting in front of him and whatnot."

"And you were married how?" Brodie snickers before turning back to the game. I study her face and see the sensation of tension in her eyes is now gone. She really did feel bad for Ben.

Damn, I just thought she was bummed about Ottawa.

**T**he buzzer sounds and the game is over. My mates are so

pissed that one of the hunky defensemen breaks a stick and it goes ricocheting, almost getting a trainer in the face. I feel for them, it's so sad to see how frustrated they are. I hope they didn't really hear what those trashy fuckers were yelling as they leave the ice. Brodie and I stand up but I tell her to wait around because I want to ask the clean up crew if I can have the broken stick.

I watch as the red neck assholes come spilling out of their row and see that the main asshole is still spouting off even though no one is there to hear him anymore. He must be drunk. As he walks passed me, he says something that finally makes me snap.

"Nice fucking Carlson jersey," he taunts.

"I hope you break your other chicken leg," I yell back at him. He keeps on walking because he's probably too pussy to get into it with me. But then his blondy pal looks at me in the eyes and decides she needs to step in.

"What did you say bitch?"

That's it.

"Why are you guys such fucking assholes?"

"We won so get over it," she retorts. I fail to see how this is related to what I had said.

"This has nothing to do with who won although your Asses haven't made the playoffs in how many years? Stop treating the players like shit, they're humans too."

"Whatever you're just mad cause we won you bitch."

"I don't care who won, I care that you guys won't shut the fuck up. Be a goddamn human."

"Your team sucks, you guys can't win shit," she keeps saying as she sways on the steps, still holding her pussy light beer. It's clear she's drunk, but I'm too angry to let that element be a reason for me to stop. I'm too pissed about everything: about my team losing, having to see the ice girls, having to listen to the team be heckled, and then being picked on myself.

"Shut the fuck up because it's clear you don't know anything about hockey otherwise you'd stop uttering the same damn phrase over and over again!"

"Whatever bitch you lost so get over yourself you dumb ho," she says again. She's still standing there and I wonder if she's a doll with a string and she's out of phrases. Why is she still standing there if she's got nothing new to say? But her calling me bitch one too many times has pissed off Brodie, who decides to step in.

"Listen here you cunt, don't talk shit about my friend with your lanky ass and think you're going to walk out of here with two legs, you'll look more like your injured douche pal if you keep at it. You probably can't even name 2 players on your own team because you're just here to be an idiot."

"Whatever I will take you on," she keeps on going with whatever energy has her still standing there facing us. Because the silent brunette recognizes Brodie's very apparent foreign element, she gets nervous and decides it's time for her to drag her dumb ass pal away. She tries to put her hand over her mouth and get her to walk backwards on the staircase. I'm banking on her to fall.

"That's right, have your drunk ass taken out of here and go blow dry your fake blonde hair," Brodie continues.

"The Partisans are losers!" she says one last time. "Just like this dumb ass comedian whose husband left her for an ice girl."

I look at Brodie. Brodie look at me. Without even saying anything out loud, we both go charging at her like Alexander Ovechkin in a shoot out. Her friend runs off like a roach and I punch blondy across the face. She falls over into a seat but manages to get up quickly.

"You bitch!" she says again, clearly not understanding that it's time to shut the fuck up before she gets punched again. This time Brodie grabs her by the hair and slaps her across the face. She falls over and we both look up to see cops coming at us. Oh shit.

# CHAPTER 21

Brodie and I spend a few hours in the slammer with a few other ladies where we explain the hilarious tale of our night. Lucky for us, these hardened women don't care at all about hockey. Otherwise I might fear that they will beat our asses for defending Ottawa.

"All things considered, I had a good time tonight. I think you and I should be better friends."

"Of course, we're the foreigner duo! I think your accent may have scared that girl a bit, as soon as she heard you weren't a Texan she was ready to drag Barbie the fuck out of there."

"Haha yeah, it sure pays to have this voice. It's a shame people can't recognize that you're a Canadian. Don't they know how enraged *Robin Scherbatsky* gets over hockey?"

"That woman is my hero, my lady," I toss my arm around Brodie's shoulder and we lean back on the hard bench.

"Alright hockey ladies, you made bail," a cop says as he unlocks the door. We both slither out and say bye to our new friends. We're feeling like total badasses, even if this will be on our permanent record.

"I hope we won't get kicked out of the country for this," I say as we go to sign some paperwork.

"Don't worry about it hun. I'm pals with the chief of police, he can clear this off. And that dumb whore isn't going to press charges if she knows what's good for her."

"I wonder who bailed us out, Ben?" I mention, then turn around to see Cory waiting in a suit down the hall.

"Cory?"

My prince ginger comes sprinting down the hall for a minute and it feels like I'm in some sexy music video where a guy longs to see his loved one after months of yearning. Then I remember I was in jail. So maybe it's a rap video and Cory's come to bail out his ho.

"Jiles! What the hell happened?"

"How did you find out?"

"Security told us what happened and said some women in the Partisans bench area got arrested for assaulting a girl. I had a sneaking suspicion it was you because, who else cares about Ottawa enough to go to jail defending them?"

"Good theory dude. And this is Brodie, she's the morning show host," I present her like a game show prize. Brodie extends her hand and smiles warmly at our night's hero. I can see she's enjoying the eye candy as much as I do.

"Thank you good sir for the tickets and for bailing us out."

"No problem, I figured it was my fault you guys came out, it was the least I could do. You guys want to tell me exactly what happened?"

**W**e recount our tale to Cory as he drives us back to our building, giving him every bit of the action and the sound effects like a lame 50's cartoon hero. Pow, boom, smack!

"I cannot believe you told her to go blow dry her hair, what the fuck was that?" I laugh my ass off in the process of reiterating what was said verbatim.

"I don't know! When I get angry I just see red and then I totally don't know what I'm saying anymore," Brodie doubles over in her own ridiculous come back, her face almost as red as Cory's hair. For having spent a few hours in jail, we are taking this evening way too lightly. To think, alcohol didn't even play a part in it! Who knew such fun could be had while being totally sober.

Cory looks over at me as I sit in the passenger seat and smiles this sincere smile, one where he's finally not giving me a look of sympathy. I can't help but feel this spark between us lately. Or maybe that's just the static electricity because I refuse to buy dryer sheets.

We park and navigate our way into the lobby of our fancy shindig, a place that Brodie is envious of. She's jealous of where I live, I'm jealous I don't get to be her.

"You guys are badasses, not gonna lie. A totally attractive quality," Cory admits as we ride up to our floor. Brodie is going to spend the night since it's late and we've had enough action for the day. Except for sexual action!

"Well Cory, what can I say, we're crazy women who love defending our team and our friends."

"I just wanted to punch a girl in the face, it's been a

while," Brodie chimes in.

"Well you ladies try to simmer down and sleep huh? No more hockey games for either of you two until your criminal record is cleared," Cory unlocks his door but decides to stand in the hall and face us like he's hoping for a three way.

"I don't think we'll be getting any sleep," I wink and open my own door. "Good night Cory," I say when Brodie steps inside. "And thank you again for tonight, you were a real hero."

"Someone who stands up for Ottawa? I think you're the hero. Good night fighter," he winks at me just before entering his own home. I'm left with the goofiest grin on my face when I go into my place. Brodie is just waiting to hear what she missed in the few seconds I had alone with Cory.

"Nothing happened, and I'd rather he not orgasm that quickly."

"I think he likes you. I think he's impressed with your need to defend your team so strongly," she says as we go into my bedroom. I pull out a pair of pajamas that fit her since we're both small ladies and we get dressed. I won't expect her to wear my pjs, she's too cool for that.

"I wish, he's too busy drooling over those ice girls too. I can hear them getting it on in there, it's such a cock tease."

"Well we should tease his cock tonight. Let's jump on the bed and moan."

Before we can make any noises or even attempt to stand up and jump, we're promptly asleep.

# CHAPTER 22

Despite feeling sparks on my *Million Dollar Baby* night, they are quickly put out because I hear it. I know Cory's on a date tonight and I'm trying so hard not to let it bother me. Just because I'm the girl next door doesn't mean all of that movie mumbo jumbo crap will come true. Besides, I have far better plans in store for moi. Tonight, the Ottawa Partisans are playing one of the most important games of the year. They're playing their longtime rivals, the Toronto Poison Ivy. This game is always super important to me. I've got beers set up, snacks, and a game starting in 10 minutes. I'm so stoked that I'm just too happy to feel any hurt about Cory. I throw on my Partisans jersey and boxers, turn off the lights, pop open a beer, and get ready for some fun.

The first period is a nightmare. The Ivy score two times on poor Pommerville, my super awesome goaltender. Every time they get one in, I shout in sheer frustration. Maybe a combination of that and knowing Cory is probably getting laid. As the period winds down, I cannot help but go into my room. I know I'll hear their conversation, if they're talking, that is. I take my beer glass and listen in.

"Do you think I'm hot?" I hear a woman's voice.

Geez, who the fuck asks a question like that? What a conceited douche.

"You're incredibly sexy Vicki," Cory compliments her.

"We'd make a perfect husband and wife. Your place is

just like mine, you're so clean. But the ice girls don't make a lot of money, and it's really not fair. We work our asses off learning routines and cleaning the ice. We're a part of the team too!"

I'm rolling my eyes so far back in my head that I half expect them to land in his bedroom.

"No yeah, I understand."

"I could be your housewife. I'd keep everything nice and clean while you're out there all sweaty and hard," she teases. At this moment I just know she's straddling him, probably with her bare breasts pressed up against his shirtless bod. He doesn't respond, I know he's turned on.

"Wouldn't you want to come home to this every single night?"

She's probably slipping her panties off at this moment.

"Absolutely," he moans in lust.

"Ooh, I know, I'll wear one of your jerseys. I bet there's nothing hotter to you than a naked girl with a hockey jersey," she says. I can hear her step aside, rummaging in his closet.

"What's this?" she asks.

"That's my old Partisans away jersey, I've had some great nights in that thing."

"There's a team called the Partisans?"

"The Ottawa Partisans? We played them last week."

"Where's Ottawa?"

I'm so mind blown at her stupidity that I go back to my living room. And just in time too, intermission is almost over. How on Earth does an ice girl who works for a team in the *National Hockey League* not know who the damn Ottawa Partisans are?!

I open a fresh beer and ready myself for period two. The period starts out great. A quick too many men on the ice penalty calls for a Partisans power play and there is some great puck dominance being shown by our 3rd line. I'm too excited to sit, perched up on my sofa, getting ready to do some hoppin' and whoopin' when my boys go for the gold.

"That's a power play goal for Ottawa, their 5th of the season," the announcer says. I jump around like a fucking kid and shout like the avid sport fan that I am. These range from, "fuck yeah," to "wahoo," "Ottawa! Ottawa! We OTTA kick your ass!" and many more. I'm probably making too much noise and interrupting their love making session. Good.

A knock. Oh great! Is a hockey player honestly going to tell me to turn it down when I'm watching hockey? I open the door and sure enough, Cory is standing there. He looks upset but not angry.

"Hey, mind if I watch the game with you?"

"How'd you know I was watching?"

"I can hear you," he laughs.

"Oh, duh. Sure," I let him in, closing the door behind me. I cleverly lock the door in case his *Spice Girl* follows. I

haven't given her a spicy name yet. I guess I'll dub her...
Whiny Spice.

"You have a lot of energy," he points out as he makes himself comfortable. I walk back, admiring his slightly worn looking Partisans old school logo tee and casual black silk shorts.

"Sorry."

"Don't be, I think it's awesome how into the game you are."

"Well I'm sorry to say that it isn't an act to get guys to think I'm cool. It's just me being me."

"And I love that about you," Cory says with sincerity as he stares at me. I'm nervous, something about the way he said that sounded far different than his normal tone. Maybe old gal pissed him off.

"Everything okay with you and Whiny Spice?"

"Uh, I guess so. I don't know. I think it might be moving too fast. I mean, she's beautiful. But that's about as far as it goes."

"I'm sure she's better than you think," I try to alter his state. I'm obviously talking out of my ass, but the least I could do is be sympathetic.

"She doesn't even know who the Partisans are," he exclaims, leaning back and plopping his socked feet on the exposed shelf of my coffee table.

"What a dumb ass. Beer?"

"Sure."

I reach into my iced metal jug of brews and pull out a favourite, *Austin Beerworks* Stout.

"A local brew, pretty damn good," I say, setting it down before him. "Help yourself to my odd array of game time snacks."

"I get the feeling watching a game here might be more fun than watching it live."

I can't help but sink in my seat just a little. That simple statement made me suddenly feel like being around me was a good thing.

Two periods pass by and I feel like it was a montage in a rom com. Partisans score again but then Toronto steals the lead before quickly gaining another goal. It seems hopeless until magically we come back and grab two goals. So now it's overtime. The entire time, we're on the edge of our seats, making far too much noise than I made on my own. We've both downed a few beers and made our way to the bottom of my snack bowls. It felt like I was hanging out with Ben in college and Ben actually cares about hockey. It's crazy to think I am experiencing this all with a former Partisan that I worshiped on the team just last year. I can only assume Whiny Spice has fallen asleep otherwise she'd be storming over here and screaming at me for stealing her date.

The entire time, Cory seems a bit different around me. Instead of being himself, I catch him looking at me in the corner of my eye. I find this surprising because this game is so important, how can he not watch? It makes me feel, dare I say? Attractive. I did happen to put on a little eyeliner today.

Furthermore, he seems to be sitting a tad closer, getting nearer after each goal. The better the Partisans do, the closer Cory gets. Maybe he has a deal where if they win, he wants me. If they lose, he blames me and chastises me forever.

Finally, our overtime period starts. We're nervous as fuck, freaking out every time Toronto has possession of the puck. We know this whole evening could be over in a second. Toronto takes a shot, Pommerville stops it. They quickly shoot again, Pommerville knocks it away with his catching glove. I'm sweating hard, pounding my breath back into regularity since my heart is in a frenzy.

And then in slow motion, it happens. Sperra grabs it. He goes for the net. He goes with a flurry of activity behind him. This is the moment, a breakaway. A chance to run from everyone as fast as you can. The chance to be a hero. Sperra shoots the puck and he swings it so hard, Reymer can't stop it. 5 hole.

The Partisans win.

"AHHHH!!" I shout as I leap up and can't contain myself. It's incredible, it's amazing, it's my first real orgasm this year! Kidding, kidding.

"That was fucking insane!" Cory smiles wider than I've ever seen. We high five and pound our fists in the air, still in awe at what a roller coaster game we've just watched.

I sit back down to collect myself and so we can watch post coverage of this incredible Partisans moment in hockey history. But before I can fixate on post coverage, I have something else to focus in on. Cory puts his hands on my face in one fell swoop, turns me to him and presses his incredibly soft lips onto mine. I'm so surprised that instead of wondering what's going on, I sink into it. I let him kiss me as much and for as long as he wants. After all, I want his lips as bad as he wants mine. He stops to breathe for a quick moment, looking into my eyes to see if I'm bothered or completely turned on. I just stare in a haze back into his eyes, half expecting to wake up.

He kisses me again but this time with more urgency. He takes his hands and puts them on my waist, slowing rising up underneath my jersey. He cups what's exposed of my breasts, pushing my bra down for more flesh to grab. In shyness, I don't touch him back at all. I just let him meander wherever he may please. Cory lets go of my breast but only to unhook my bra. Now that the obstacle has been cleared, he is completely grabbing hold of them, giving me a reason to tremble like I had during overtime. I take a peak down and see that along his black silk shorts, his penis is hard and hoping to pull a Sperra overtime goal himself.

Damn me: this is an opportunity of a life time. This was something I would dream of long before I even knew Cory personally. This is something I would love to pull to get back at the type of women that destroyed my marriage. Yet still, I decide I have to do the responsible thing. I pull back and push him off, lightly of course.

"What's wrong?" he asks, catching his breathe and speaking slow.

"There's a girl in your apartment," I point out, fingers and everything.

"Oh. The thing is, I don't want to be with her. She's an idiot. You're your own woman. You're funny as fuck, you're strong willed, determined, smart, independent."

I cannot help but notice something, he hasn't called me attractive. He only lists my traits. Should I be hurt by this?

"And I don't know why it took me this long to see it, but you're goddamn beautiful."

There it is. Now I am smiling wide, but I have to remain focused.

"This isn't right. You were on a date tonight and now you're making out with me."

"Why are you worried about her? I thought you of all people hated the ice girls."

"I do, but there's a reason. I don't fuck a chick's man."

Cory nods, gathering exactly why I was turning down this rare moment to get with him. It's because I would not stoop to their level.

"I completely respect that," he stands himself up. "I guess I'd better go," he points to the door like a hitch hiker before he sees himself out. I watch the embarrassment in his eyes as well as his still very erect penis go out the door. Aw shucks.

I sit in my spot with no energy to get up, turned on so bad I almost want to call him and toss my morals out on the terrace. But I'm a good kid, so instead I go to my bedroom and do the mature thing. I get naked and rub one out. And as it turns out, Zach Galifianakis' character in *Due Date* was right. I did have me un glorious orgasm-o and slept like a baby.

# CHAPTER 23

Besides my DVD taping, there's nothing going on in my life. I have no plans, I haven't seen Cory since the awkward interaction, and Ben has been busy with *ACL* promotional events galore. Or maybe it's a cover up because he's still uncomfortable around me. I would go despite all of this drama but I don't want to because it half involves watching football. I do attend a work out session with Brodie three times this week. She's committed to being my trainer, my mother if you will. I think it's because she doesn't have kids and she's nearing 40. But she's certainly a *MILF* if I swung that way! I follow her routine, vowing to eating healthier even if it's detrimental to my lunch dates with Ben. All in all, I would say I'm shaping my life up good. I'm doing everything but trying to date and getting passed my seething hatred of the ice girls. Let's be honest here, that's probably never going to happen. I hear a knock on my door and wonder if it's Cory, hoping he'll stop by since it's been a few weeks.

"JILES!" the door busts open without so much as a twist of the knob. It is my mother...in law. My mother is in Winnipeg on a road trip! Is she still welcome?

"Aren't you supposed to hate me?" I point out right in during her obligatory squeeze. Damn her old lady perfume, I can hardly breathe.

"Of course not darling!" she coos in her rich, suburban voice. She is the prototype of a rich mother. Mushroom shaped hair only a woman past 60 can pull off in a blonde that only comes from boxes at the salon. Wrinkles that are subtly hidden by the greatest products on the market. A white blazer and slacks, shoes only old ladies seem to find, and let's not forget her Diane Keaton gloves. This lady, what a trip.

"Jiles, Frank and I miss you so much!" she wallows, taking a seat at my island. She has been here a few times before. If not this would be even weirder.

"I'm sorry," I apologize as if any of this were my doings.

"I feel like such a terrible mother. How could I raise a son that leaves a wonderful woman like you after years of courtship for some hussy!" she laments, grief so stricken on her face that I completely believe for once that she likes me. Better late than never, eh?

"It's not your fault, Mrs. Richardson. You can't control the decisions your son makes."

"He's obviously an idiot then. I just can't believe it. We want you back!"

"I'm afraid that isn't an option," I snicker, searching my scrambled mind for the right thing to say. This conversation feels more awkward than when I first met her.

"We met her last week, it was awful. She was so stupid!" She drags out stupid like 'steeuuupidd.' "She didn't go to college, doesn't have any plans post this job that will last her until she's 30. She wore far too much make up, more than me for christ sakes!"

I can't help but laugh. No one outdoes this lady on

make up. It's a full on burlesque/drag show on this lady's face.

"I can't imagine having to deal with that tramp at holidays and family reunions. But worst of all, I don't want that woman being the mother of my grandchildren. We love you so much Jiles. You were the perfect woman. Educated, hard working, determined, loyal."

"I really appreciate that, thanks."

"And their children are going be so ugly with both of them being so pretty and all. You and Ford would have made gorgeous children!"

Barely a split second passes before I realize this is an insult, glaring at her before I decide I'll just let it go.

"I mean...well you know what I mean."

"I know. I'm no ice girl."

"No, you aren't. You're my girl," she puts her hand on top of mine. Her silk glove is quite comforting. I spent a lot of holidays with this woman. For example, since we celebrate Thanksgiving in Canada in October, I've spent every Thanksgiving for the past 5 years with them. When I couldn't fly home for Christmas, I was at their West Lake house. I spent so many familial occasions with this woman and now I've become the ghost of holiday's past.

"Tell me you'll still celebrate Thanksgiving with us?" she asks.

"I don't think Ford would appreciate that."

"Yeah well..." she leans her body on the table before removing her elbows. She's quick to display her old fashion manners. "Fuck him, it's my house."

"Haha, okay."

There is still no way I'll come over, but I appreciate her sticking up for me and not her own son. That's some real motherly love shit alright. Got the in-laws on my side: I win.

"What are you doing this evening Jiles?" she asks me. I'm under the impression that she thinks I'm going to go out with her like we're old ladies chatting it up with tea and some overpriced, nicely cut sandwiches.

"I'm going to rehearse my special actually."

"Splendid, I'll join you! It'll be a girls night out, let's go get a drink to loosen you up!"

She hugs me again and despite how displeased I am with this situation, I'm thankful that someone out there gives a shit about me beside Brodie and Ben. I guess I could use a mother around here. Plus, it will really piss off *Kia Rio*.

**M**y practice goes good and while I wait for light cues and sounds to go along, I look at my phone and see that Cory has scored 2 goals. He's waiting for a hat trick and probably on his knees in excitement. This statement is ripe for a dirty line but I don't feel like thinking of one. It's your turn to work your dirty mind. And you can't tell me you don't have a dirty mind otherwise you'd have stopped reading this ages ago!

In lieu of our mutually good nights, I wonder if we will

have an interaction afterwards. I head on home after we get our timing done and *Mitsubishi's* mom says goodbye. I'm sure she's excited to go home and tell all of her girlfriends about what a fun night on the town she had with a woman half her age. She will use this card as her cool element for as long as it runs. I wouldn't be surprised if she's even hidden my divorce from her posse. There's no way she'd want them to know about she lost her celebrity connection for a cheerleader.

Wait a minute, let me just clarify here. I respect cheerleaders, the real ones. The ones that do all of those crazy spins, twirls, stacking on other people. That's some real talented stuff right there. But these ice girls, they just kind of dance around with a pom pom and don't do anything worth watching unless you're wanting a boner. So why are they given the same category when actual cheerleading competition is far more extreme and respected? I ponder this on the way to dinner. But if you think I'm a bitch, me saying this now won't change anything will it?

I decide to eat at my favourite place again, *Zen,* since they are still open this late. The place is empty and I'm sure the employees are mad that I'm here so I slip them all a $20 as a thank you tip. They toss some smiles on their faces and even give me my soda for free. I sit and stare out at busy, bustling Guadalupe, watching the cars pass by rapidly as I wonder who these people are and what they are doing. I check my phone again and see the game is over. Cory has indeed gotten his hat trick and no surprise there, they won.

"Congrats," I text him, deciding one of us should break the ice and get over our last interaction.

"Thanks," Cory responds halfway through my meal. He attaches a photo of the guys locker room and wouldn't you believe it? They are partying like motherfuckers in there. You'd think they'd clinched a playoff spot.

"Gonna go get drunk?"

"I'm sure of it. Come with?"

I quickly run through my head why this isn't a good idea. Drinking, hockey players, and my show tomorrow. Does this really need to happen? I get the feeling I might wind up in a *Hangover* type situation and get lost in Bangkok, missing out on my opportunity of a life time to make my own DVD.

"I think I'm good, I don't want to be hungover for my taping."

"Holy shit, I forgot it was tomorrow. Am I still invited?"

Did me denying him sex negate his invitation? I let him stew for a few minutes before I reply. Maybe he'll think that I'm cautiously debating this because I have morals and want my show to be pristine. The truth is I'm just doing this to be an ass.

"Of course," I add while taking a bite of my awesome shrimp bowl with veggies and noodles galore. Oh so savory and quite nutritious too, Brodie would be proud of my healthy meal.

It's 3 in the morning when I hear banging on the wall behind my head. What the hell?

"Jiles," I hear a muffled voice. He knocks on the wall

again. "Jiles?"

I decide to use this rare opportunity to rip off a great joke by the late and great Mitch Hedberg. "Go around!"

I guess he listened because I hear knocking coming from my front door. I walk over and unlock it, picking out the crust in my eyes as I shuffle around in my moose jammies.

"Jiles, are you awake?" he asks. Oh boy is he lit! If I can't pick that up from his state, I certainly can't miss it from his smell.

"No I'm a zombie. Dude it's like 3am," I yawn, looking my worst and caring my least.

"Sorry, I'm drunk!"

"I can tell."

"Can I spend the night?"

"Why?"

"I don't want to be alone, I'm too happy."

I close the door behind him and take his hand, leading him to my bedroom. He jumps on my bed as soon as he can, bouncing high enough that I think he'll hit his head on the ceiling.

"Down boy," I command him like a dog, patting the side of the bed for him to come down to. He immediately listens but still holds his very energetic stance. "Lay down."

He listens to this instruction as well. I go to my side and climb aboard, making sure I leave a decent distance in case I decide to take advantage of his state.

"I love your pajamas, you are so cute," he giggles, tossing the covers over himself.

"How much did you drink?"

"I don't even know anymore, I just know I had a great fucking time and the guys got me in a cab home."

"Well, I'm glad you had a good night."

"It would have been better if you were there."

I look at him with what light is available. His tender lips are curved up in a smile that can only be drawn on a *Charlie Brown* character. His eyes glow their blue hue and illuminate my soul because goddamn is he happy and it's spreading over to me. How infectious his good mood is!

"You're the coolest girl ever. I wish you would have come. No woman in town would have appreciated tonight like you would have. I'm sorry this didn't happen while I was in Ottawa."

"Hey, better late than never," I say but know I'm not really thinking. My heart is pounding bad because he's so hot.

"Are you mad at me?" he interjects. Oh alcohol, I love how blunt you make people.

"Not at all."

"I thought you were mad at me because I tried to sleep with you."

I should tell him I said no because I have chlamydia; he's so drunk he won't remember. But maybe I should just be serious for once.

"I'm not mad, I was just nervous. I always want to do the right thing, even if it means disappointing people and myself."

"That's great, no you're awesome. You're so awesschoome," he slurs, spinning his head around the room in a funny attempt to probably loosen his neck. "I like being around you, you're funny and cool. It's like a high school sleepover in here."

"I'm glad I remind you of an under age girl. Now let's get some sleep, eh?"

"Okay babe. I cannot wait for your show tomorrow. It's gonna be so awesome. You're going to tell three amazing jokes and I'm going to toss a Partisans hat on the stage."

"I would actually love that," I laugh, cozing up as I face him, sheets covering me up just below my nose.

"Boop!" he touches my nose with a poke of his warm index finger.

I laugh my ass off at this super cute move. He's still smiling and laughing like we're innocent children. I'm in love with this moment, truly.

"Good night Jiles, I love you."

"Love you too man," I respond even if I'm not sure what element he says these words in. He closes his eyes still in his smile, nestling his head into my pillow. All I can think about is how bad I want to kiss him but in his child like state, it would feel like statutory rape.

I wake up earlier than normal, post the live morning show that is. There's no way I would ever wake up at five in the morning on my own! I have completely forgotten about the hunky ginger in my bed, so I let out a slight 'gah' and shake when I roll over and see his body. When I remember last night, I slink into a girly fascination as I admire his features with no worries that I will be caught. His face is absolutely delicious, and his lips just seem like the tastiest things on the market. I wonder if he has morning wood and because I have no morals, I lift up the sheets to take a peak. He doesn't. Rats.

Subliminal messages suddenly pop into my thoughts. Do those things really work? I head to *iTunes* on the ole cellular device and purchase a copy of Avril Lavigne's *Girlfriend*. Ya know, that one where she wants to be someone's girlfriend and that the guy's current girl is a total douche? It seems fitting, don't it?

I put the song on and slide my phone below his pillow so that it isn't directly playing into his ear. I decide to get up and fix us some coffee, grabbing some aspirin and water too. I know sleeping beauty will need a cure for his very due hangover. I also go out and quickly pick up some *Shipley's* kolaches, the best goddamn donut shop in the world.

As I'm stepping into my room I hear music...oh shit! I accidentally put the song on loop! I quickly snag it away and turn the song off. Poor Cory, no one should be forced to listen to a pop song on loop for 30 minutes. Not even for mind bending purposes.

Cory wakes up to the sight of me downing a sausage and cheese kolache like I'm giving it head, cracking a smile.

"Morning," I mutter while chewing. I reach for the bag and set it before him. "If you haven't had one yet, it will be love at first bite. *Dunkin' Donuts* is nothing compared to this Texas tradition," I explain to him. He sits up and reaches in, taking a bite and I see his own surprise at how damn good it is.

"Holy Hannah that's amazing," he swallows.

"There's some aspirin and water, I suggest you take it now before the hurt sets in."

He quickly does so, finishing his first kolache in the process. While chewing he looks around my room and admires my Ottawa pendants on the wall, and my moose family. I haven't introduced him to them yet. But I don't think I'm ready to let him know I have 13 French Canadian moose doll children.

"Am I going crazy or were you listening to an Avril Lavigne cd?"

"Me? Ha, listening to pop music. That's rich," I gulp and look away. Do do do do do....

"How stupid was I last night?" he asks, clearly embarrassed to be waking up in my bed.

"Not at all, it was funny and cute. It was nice having

company."

"At any rate, I am sorry. I must have woken you up last night. And I hope I didn't vomit anywhere."

"No, you didn't. If you did it would be on *eBay* right now so. Hockey player vomit is like a currency in Canada."

He laughs silently as he eats a second one.

"These are great, thank you for taking care of me last night. You're the only family I have here it seems."

"That's not true, you've got your boys. Those Austin Ass-assins peoples," I spout off before finishing my breakfast.

"Yeah but, you took me in while I was stupid and drunk and got me food? No one has done that for me in a long ass time. Thanks," he puts his hand on my shoulder and rubs me much like a tongue would circle an ice cream scoop. "I suppose I should let you get ready for your show tonight. You must be nervous."

"I am actually, it's been a long time since I've been nervous about performing."

"It's only healthy. So, be there at 6pm right? Dressed better than a post game?"

"No suit required," I nod my head. "I'll slip you a ticket below your door."

"Just one?"

"Did you need more?" I say with no emotion even if

I'm secretly bothered.

"No, I don't," he tricks me.

He gets up and looks down to make sure he's not poking, looking back up with a silly grin that he gave me last night. Maybe that really is his smile, not just a drunk trait. Maybe I broke a barrier between us and now I'm seeing more of the real him. He salutes me as he walks out, neither of us tossing in a last word to ruin the lingering sexy connotation of his last comment.

# CHAPTER 24

The time has finally arrived after the slow passing of the day, just making me even more nervous for every slow tick of my inner clock.

It's here. The night I'm going to lose my virginity.... my stand up DVD virginity! Brodie came over early and took me to a salon again, she insists I don't look like shit tonight. I told her there was no way I could look like shit since I'll be the only person seen on the DVD, therefore no one to compare me with.

"You look gorgeous!" Brodie exclaims, showing me a hand mirror to see what her hair stylist has done for me. I have it all: volume, sleek strands, and bounce. I look like a whore, but I like it. Does that mean I like looking like a whore? Yes, yes it does.

"Brod, isn't it funny how looking good means looking more like a fucking ice girl?" I ask in disdain for this fact.

"Hun, just because you look pretty doesn't mean you aren't still you. And that's what's important, right?"

I accept her words of wisdom as she takes me over to someone who will do my make up. I'm wearing some knee high black boots and a black dress. It's a bit too tight for me, but it's showing my goods as best as they can be presented. You know, like when they dress up a shitty fast food sandwich for the ad but it never looks that good in person.

A woman starts tossing foundation on my face, along with other colours and items that I have no idea what they are. I know a little about this, but not enough to care to watch and learn. I suppose a part of me expects to get this luxury treatment for as long as I'm a relevant comedian, so why bother? As soon as you make money, you start going to places where someone carries your luggage, escorts you on an elevator, and hands you tissue to wipe your ass like you never knew how to do anything before. And then when I go broke I can be a baby and whine that no one is mothering me. Kind of like people from New Jersey trying to get gas when they leave their state and discover that no one is going to do it for them.

"You're going to be fabulous tonight, Jiles."

"Ben isn't coming is he?" I finally ask a question I've been meaning to ask but didn't think I could stomach the response. I haven't heard from him or seen him the day after we fucked. I admit it, my feelings are hurt. He promised me that wouldn't affect our friendship and yet he has headed for the hills.

"He said he has something to say to you. He's here, don't you worry your pretty little head. He wouldn't bail on tonight."

Brodie gives me as much of a hug as she can while I am gussied up for my taping. She already looks damn good herself, always in the know of what's cool to wear and what make up to try on. And that hairstyle she's rocking? Maybe it's not such a bad idea because you don't have to do much beside toss some gel in. But me cut my hair that short? I don't need to look even more like a man!

When I'm done, she snaps a few pictures and I entertain

her by actually posing too. No duck lips though, please! I'd like to have a shred of dignity left after my stint as a *YouTube* sensation. Instead I do my siggy smile, the muppet face. All smiley mouth, no teeth!

We head off in a provided town car and they take us down to the *Paramount Theatre*, dropping me off at the back door where I'm ushered in along with my crew. Inside, Brodie finds Ben, who is waiting around and talking to more promotional do-gooders. They were both gifted with VIP badges since they did so much promotional giveaway for my show. Ben is surprisingly dressed nice, in a blue button up shirt with white pinstripes and black pants that fit snugly on his bum. Even more of a shocker, he has flowers!

"Jiles, can I talk to you for a second?" he asks me.

"Sure."

Ben puts his hand on the small of my back and walks with me to a more private area. I expect him to be quivering with fear to say something I don't want to hear but he looks more relaxed than me.

He provides me the goofy grin he always gave me anytime I needed coaxing in my career. "You're going to be alright kid," he would always say. The fact that he always smiled made me feel like he was always right; it never worried him in the slightest, smiling as naturally as he felt my life would pan out.

"Um, I just wanted to tell you that I'm so happy for you. After all of those years, you really have made it. And I know tonight is a big night for you and despite all of the shit that you've been through, you'll get over it."

"You've been avoiding me?" I say point blank.

"Brodie told you huh?"

"Duh, she has a vagina."

"Look, I was afraid I liked you okay!" he looks away and gnaws on his lower lip. I've never seen this side of him before. I feel pity. I never wanted things to get like this. "I wanted to make damn sure I got over anything I thought I was feeling because the last thing you need to be in is another relationship. I'm a terrible boyfriend and you deserve better than me because I don't want to be in a relationship with anyone. And if you started liking me, that would be bad too. You are my best friend Jiles. We don't need none of that dating nonsense getting in the way of our already clogged arteries."

I can't help but laugh. Damn Ben is funny.

"What we have now, I love it. You're my best fucking friend and that's way better than getting in your pants."

"The fact that you've put my feelings ahead of my pussy is very touching. I know how much you like sex, so I really do feel the sincerity of this. I love you too Ben, and you're absolutely right. Like I said, you're the only dude in this whole country I trust. I can't risk losing that over a quick fuck. But...we should make that 40 pack, if we're both single thing!"

"I see that happening so sure! But if I need you and I'm desperate, you're available now, right?"

"Haha, maybe, I think things are on the up and up with hockey boy," I wink.

"Here you go," he smiles, handing me flowers. Ben looks so incredible. Even if he is overweight, his charm and his kindness always far exceed whatever his body looks like.

"Thanks babe, and you clean up nice my dear," I bow and courtesy.

"As do you, and I can only assume these are Brodie's doings since you'd never do this shit yourself," Ben inquires, taking notice of my hair and make up.

"Of course, you know I have no idea what I'm doing in any part of my life!"

"Good luck tonight, Jiles," he hugs me, squeezing me as he lifts me up even, too damn strong for me to fight him.

Ben and Brodie go out to the front row where I got them some kick ass seats along with other important folk in my life, which is no one. Except for Cory of course, who is wearing a crisp pair of black pants with folds in them like they're new, black shiny shoes and a navy button up shirt with a black tie. He's sitting next to Brodie, so hopefully she will both entertain him and keep him in check in case he tries to flirt with another girl at my damn show. I see him shake hands with Ben, who from the looks of it is apologizing for being such an asshole during the show. I feel so warm about Ben's kind words, knowing my friendship with him will indeed last me a lifetime.

Canon rushes to the front row, last minute as I assume she was busy primping herself. She sits next to Cory and introduces herself to the others. By the way, this is the first time I've ever seen her not in her gear. I must say, she still looks very beautiful.

The producers tell me to go stand to the left of the red velvet curtains where I will nervously await the moment. I think about how people willingly entered a theatre where the bright marquee said "Austin's Canadian: Jiles Perry" and wonder if someone changed it to say someone worthy of bringing this many people in. I analyze every inch of the atmosphere, admiring the golden polish of the balcony down to the doors that spill into the orchestra. Sparkles of the bright white lights hurt my eyes a tad and make it hard for me to scrutinize the people pouring into the room. People linger in the balcony seating, standing around and chatting it up while random music plays overhead. They start to quiet down as the lights changes their opacity, dimming down over their heads to let them know it's time to shut the fuck up and pay attention to me. Oh shit! I suddenly hear over the entire building...

"Ladies and gentleman, Austin's Canadian, Jiles Perry!"

*"I'm Your Torpedo,"* by *Eagles of Death Metal* begins to play as I walk out in a silly strut to the centre of the stage. I can't even believe how many people are in the room, my biggest audience yet. My heart is pounding for no stage fright at all. It's because I know Cory Koenig is here to watch me perform for the first time. My mother in law is here. And I'm pretty sure Ford and that tramp are here too. I gave her a second pair of tickets and I know she'd try to get Ford to come and see what a fool he was to dump a star on the rise.

"AUSTIN!" I shout. "I like how I have to pretend I'm just here on a tour but in reality I fucking live here!"

I get a vast array of applause, whistles and loud Bronx cheers from my fans and anyone else that stumbled in this evening. It's coming from every corner of this room I'm facing. The high vaulted ceilings with their Roman empire reminiscence help echo this back, sounding louder than ever. Maybe I'm wrong; I'm no scientist. I don't understand sound theory or speed of light. I just know my heart is pumping and everything is zooming passed me like I'm on a rocket to outer space, full speed ahead. Choo choo!

"How are ya'll doing tonight? That's right, I'm from Canada and I say ya'll now. Fuck me I've converted, eh? But I miss my home. In fact, a little bit o' home came to me. My neighbor hails from my hometown hockey team and it has been a blast getting to talk to someone from Ottawa. Except, I can hear him fucking all the time, and it just sucks because it reminds me of how much I'm not getting laid.

I wanted to one up him, so I went online and found this one porno. I watched it so many damn times until I knew exactly when this dude moaned the woman's name right? Then one night when I knew he was home, I played it really loudly while I jumped on my bed, and I muted it every time he moaned her name and inserted my own."

*"Oh yeah, you like that dick-"*

Mute."Jiles!"

*"You are so fucking hot-"*

Mute. "Jiles!"

*"I know you love this, yeah, you love this dick up your ass-"*

Mute. "Jiles! No wait, I mean no, get it the fuck out! Get it the fuck out!"

The audience laughs wholeheartedly at my new joke, and I even spot Cory laughing too. That felt good. I wonder if he thinks I did for for real?

"I got dolled up today so that horny old men will jerk off to this DVD. Normally I went around looking like shit because I was married and didn't care. And then my husband left me and so now I'm free to fuck the world. I think I'll get funnier when I start having more fuck stories to share with you. Like I boned a hockey player and it was a Canadian girl's dream come true. We used maple syrup as lube even. But it got sticky in all of my pubes because I stopped shaving when I got divorced and that was almost a year ago."

Laughter. Oh sweet laughter how I love thee. I hope I made Ford cringe.

"I love red headed men, I think they're sexy as fuck. I don't care how ugly or fat they are, you have those flamy locks I'd do ya. I have no standards, I fucked Ben White," I say and point to him. People are losing their shit and Ben isn't offended one bit. I ran the joke by him and he loved it!

"The problem for me is, the redder a guy's hair, the younger they are! So I end up hitting on guys and then I quickly find out they are underage. I saw this one guy at the mall coming out of a *Hot Topic* and I said one word to him before being taken away in cuffs. I guess I should have known he was underage, coming out of a *Hot Topic*. I haven't been there since I grew pubes!"

The audience roars with laughter and it warms up my soul to hear it. Every time I hear those sounds, cackles, guffaws, those every things that mean I made someone smile within, it does the trick. It also means I am a step closer to breaking out of my divorce depression. Knowing I can make someone happy by sharing a story from my life is better than anything I could ever feel. I'm talking love, wealth, sex. Nothing could compare to the high I feel when I make someone laugh.

**T**hat's all for me, thank you very much! Good night Austin!" I thank the audience as Buffalo Speedway's *"War"* plays for my outro song. Everyone applauses, a few even stand up. I think it's a local thing since they all knew me from my small steps at open mic nights for years. I smile and wave at everyone, making eye contact with Ben, Brodie, Cory, and Canon. Then my eyes zoom in on the unthinkable. Ford is indeed here with his 'rents. Unbelievable. I bow and try to press this new information out of my mind for this last incredible moment of my biggest night yet.

I get back stage and take a glass of water where the tech crew dudes are all high five-ing me and telling me how much I rocked the night. I'm completely smitten with the happiness of this night, but seeing Ford has messed that all up. And just as I know there is a reason he is here, I see him come into the back room. He obviously stole one of the VIP passes I gave his mom. This guy just loves to toss his relationship drama into my comedy break through salads. First my tour and now this.

"Jiles!" he smiles at me, as if smiling at me is anything but appropriate.

"Yea?" I hold back no hesitation in my complete disdain for this occurrence.

"Can we talk?"

"What the hell are you doing here man?"

Ford sighs, knowing it won't be easy to get me to ease up on him. Of course not, why the hell should I be nice? Did I bombard the night of his life after I left him?

"Jiles, you were incredible this evening. I'm so proud of you."

"Okay, thanks. What the hell are you doing here?" I question again, pointing a booted foot at him and tapping as I wait for whatever his stupid reasonings are.

"I think I made a mistake. You and I have been something else, and I can't figure out why I let that go," he admits. Ford takes a hand through though his caramel brown hair that has gotten longer, almost in an 80's shag. He wears a gray suit like only a West Lake richie boy would wear. He's so *Miami Vice* I want to gouge my eyes out in his fail to be cool look. "You look so gorgeous, Jiles."

"You left me, Ford. You left a box of our memories in our apartment, that was your final fuck you. Am I right?" I hold nothing back, shouting decibels higher than my last question. My hands are shaking and I know I've got the face of *Oscar the Grouch* going on. I'm full on muppet mode: pissed off and animated in my movement, except the only thing puppeteer-ing my arms are the pulse-y twitches of the nerves that have had it up to here with this guy. Or maybe Ford's fist is up my ass, which is what this moment feels like. An unwelcome fuck you through my backstage entrance.

"No, I left that there because I couldn't decide who deserved those more, you or me. And in the end, I wanted you to have our pieces because I sure as hell didn't deserve them. You were always faithful and good to me, and I'm the one that ruined everything. I don't think I made a mistake, I know I made a mistake."

I look passed him to see Cory coming in the room. He smiles at me until he sees the razor sharp hurt in my eyes. His happiness drops in his concern, realizing a state of mine he's never seen.

"Are you okay?" he asks before even noticing that Ford is right before him.

"Oh, is he your...?" Ford asks, pointing to Cory with a bit of surprise that someone that attractive is talking to me.

"No, this is one of my friends from back home. Cory, this is Ford," I hesitate to tell him, grinding my teeth and shuffling my feet.

"Oh," he immediately figures out why I'm so upset. "Do you need a moment?"

"Yeah, I'll come talk to you in a second."

He leans down to whisper in my ear, "you can tell him I'm your boyfriend if you want." Before he steps aside, I look up at him and see the warmth in his eyes intertwined with his sorrow for this truly icky situation I'm about to be in. He's team Jiles' coach and I'm about to enter overtime. This is his strategy, to remind me I'm stronger and I can win this game against my biggest enemy.

Coach Cory walks away and I hesitate to start again until he makes the first peep.

"I think-"

"Look Ford, it's too late."

"But Jiles."

"Don't do this to me man. You did this to me. You and that fucking *Spice Girl*, and things aren't working out and you figured out she was only after your money but guess what? I was only after your heart and you fucking broke mine instead! You can't come back from your quick fuck and expect me to get over it thinking I'm desperate because I'm not! That guy over there, that's Cory Koenig! He is a mother fucking former Ottawa Partisan AND he digs me. Guess what? I boned a Vancouver Moose and he was insanely awesome. I even drunk fucked Ben and guess what? It was.... mediocre but it sure as hell felt better to fuck people that didn't dump me for a cheerleader. So no, I won't be with you again because you showed me your true colours, dude bro! I'll keep in contact as friends but that's it."

He stays quiet for a moment as everything I say sinks in. I'm not at all who he thinks I am anymore, I'm learning to come out of my lonely spell and hang out with the likes of people he never thought would give me the time of day. I've grown out of our comfortable former ways and found such a better world outside of that.

"I completely understand Jiles, and I respect that. I just thought, I had to give it a shot, right?" he whimpers as if I'm supposed to feel sorry for him. And strangely enough, I do. That's who I am, I can't yell at people without feeling remorse. I can't do unto others the hurt they have done to me. But for once, I'm putting my big ole clown feet down. Red floppy shoes and all.

"Yeah, and I respect that. But it doesn't change all of the hurt you caused me. You're welcome to come to the after party if you'd like," I roll my eyes. I know, I shouldn't have said that, but I'm always the bigger person.

"I'd like that, yeah. My parents will be there too anyway. By the way, they asked me to beg you to still come for holidays. I know that's weird, but I feel like we're all still family you know?"

"Your mom asked me. I'll think about it," I say and this time, I mean it. Despite this unnecessary drama, I know within what tonight really is and how everything is going to get better for me. So why not let go of the things that hurt and spread the joy, even to those that don't deserve it from me?

"The party is just across the street, here," I hand him some passes from my purse. Yes, I do have a stack of them. I should have just thrown them off the patio, it would have been a faster way to get rid of them.

"By the way, I'm sorry I made you feel dumb about your moose dolls. I think in the end, it was just a sign that you would have been an excellent mother to our children. I was just too stupid to realize that at the time," Ford smiles at me fondly and steps away back in the sea of the audience, where he now belongs in my life.

Ah crap, why is he trying to fill my head with that feeling like we're meant to be together? Cory comes up to me immediately and takes my hand.

"Hey, are you okay?"

"I don't know," I stammer, feeling ready to cry but

nothing comes out.

"What did he say?" Cory asks with more enthusiasm than I expected. I sense jealously, which I totally approve of.

"He wanted me to take him back."

"Oh," he looks away, giving me a moment to explain my response.

"I said no."

"Good for you, it's his turn to be hurt. Come here," he hugs me tightly, giving me a great whiff of his warm body and that comfortable scent everyone carries with themselves. Cory rocks me with his uber muscular arms and it's in his grasp that I know I'm safe from the emotional outburst I just ensued. Meeting and befriending someone that I thought would never talk to me just helps frost my cake of the future. I'm talking tiramisu, the tastiest shit on the market.

# CHAPTER 25

Cory, Canon, Brodie, Ben and I hop into my town car and they take us just a block over. I know we could have walked, but I'm lazy and so is my posse. We step inside of the hotel where my party is being hosted on the penthouse and go up. None of us need to show our credentials, which may be even better than the warm feeling of making people laugh. Oh no, I'm turning into a spoiled asshole.

Some crew members are already there, as well as some of the audience that I gave passes to. Mrs. Richardson spots me and waltzes up to me as fast as an old lady can, arms open to hug me.

"Jiles! You were amazing tonight!"

"Thanks, mom," I utter before realizing it's inappropriate to call her that.

"Did Ford talk to you?"

"Yes, he did."

"What did you say?" she covers her mouth, waiting for the results like a teenager watching *American Idol*. Aw man, I gotta disappoint two people tonight?

"I'm sorry, but I've moved on. He hurt me, and I can't forget it. But I will be cordial, be friends."

"And you'll still come spend holidays with us?"

"And I'll spend holidays with you."

"GOOD!" she smiles like I'm telling her I'm pregnant with her grandkids. As if that would ever happen, no kids for me! Unless they are in the form of cute moose dolls.

While she hugs me again, I look around and see that Cory isn't waiting behind me anymore. I see Ben getting drinks with Canon and Brodie hob nobbing with some fancy suited audience members who probably recognize her. I will laugh my ass off if Ben tries to hit on Canon. He said he would never sleep with an ice girl but I would love to see this hilarity unfold. If anything, it would make for an amazing story for the morning show!

Instead of wondering where Cory has gone off to I go around the room and take photos with people, signing a few autographs even, just being a general cool person in Austin. An hour has passed by when I suddenly see Cory coming up to me with a huge smile on his face and I'm completely surprised. It's like he has good news for me. He approaches me when I'm in the distance a bit, admiring a crowd of my viewers.

"You wouldn't believe it Jiles," Cory shakes in head in bewilderment. "That ice girl, Katie, she came onto me in the same room as your ex husband!"

"Oh? Well everyone says she's hot."

"What a horrible woman! Who home wrecks and then flirts with other people in the same room at YOUR party! You would never do some shit like that. You had the chance and you said no."

"What can I say? I'm a good Canadian with a heart o' gold," I prance my arm like a leprechaun and do a little step with it too. Cory smiles and laughs, still grinning that gorgeous look I saw since day one.

"Jiles, your show was awesome. You were hilarious. And if you don't mind me saying, you look insanely beautiful tonight," he says, getting closer to me and directing his words so that only I can hear them. I fear he is embarrassed to let anyone hear him compliment me, but then I decide it sounds so quiet because only I can hear it. Maybe it's because they are the best words that ever come out of his mouth and I want them all to myself. I don't need a mirror to know I'm gushing. I look down as I try to figure out the right words. I need a joke, a joke Jiles, quick!

"No one has ever said insanely to me before, unless they were telling me I was insanely drunk."

"Well I mean it. Yeah, that Katie is a piece of work."

"What did you say to her?"

"I told her, she may have taken Ford Richardson from the funniest chick in Austin," he steps closer and leans down a bit so that his nose is inching closer to me. Is he going to peck me like a bird? "But, she's not taking Cory Koenig from the funniest and hottest chick in Austin. Of course, I didn't say that in third person," he laughs and leans in the last bit to feel my lips against his.

"If it's okay with you," he whispers in a husky breath into my ear. "I'd like to pick up where we left off when you used your better judgment and I did not. Although I can't say wanting to kiss you was bad judgment."

Between him telling me I'm hot, him breathing down my ear creating mad chills, and that kiss? I'm just waiting for him to ravish me.

"My place or yours?"

"Does it matter? As long as it's with you," he kisses me again.

We sally forth immediately like two agents on a secret mission, down the long elevator ride and ushered into my town car. Within minutes as the venue isn't too far away, we're back to our respective pads.

"Bad news folks," the door man says. "The elevator is down again."

Cory and I look at each other with disgust as we start our journey up 14 flights of stairs.

"I'm sorry to say I probably won't be able to perform by the time we get up there," I joke halfway through our jaunt.

We finally get up to our floor and I unlock my door as Cory stands eagerly behind me. We enter my bedroom and as I turn to face Cory, he's already taking his shirt off and smiling the sexiest, most horny grin I've ever seen.

"God you're sexy Jiles. I'm so sorry I didn't realize that the second I laid eyes on you," he drools as he eyes me taking off my dress.

"I'm no ice girl."

"You're right. You'd melt that shit in a heartbeat."

I slip out of my bra and panties while Cory takes off his boxers. If this is what all of the hockey players look like, no wonder they all marry so young. Hubba Hubba.

Cory and I step closer to each other and he puts his hands on my waist, grabbing me even to the point I'd say he's digging in too much. He somehow manages all of the strength in just his hands to lift me and lay me on the bed, quickly assuming missionary position.

He gazes into my eyes and even though it's dark, we can still manage to make out our features thanks to some moonlight pouring into my uncovered window. His gingerly hair is especially shining in radiance.

"Why would someone leave you behind?" he flatters me, kissing my forehead and my cheeks.

"I'm sorry about Kal, I don't want to be a rink rat," I admit.

"Could you not tell how jealous I was?" Cory finally admits. His tone is so dire that it seems this situation ate him up inside.

"A little, but you had never said anything about me in that regard so I wasn't willing to pass up a chance to feel good about my body again."

Instead of a witty retort, he begins to kiss me lightly before laying his lips on my neck. "Cory," I coo as he warms my nerves to a point of complete relaxation.

His hands are grazing my hard nipples now, kissing them even. Yowza! Before I know it, he's pressing his penis inside my very lubed up opening and the real *Schlitterbahn* water park ride for cocks begins. But instead of this being a fun quickie session, Cory makes it real. It lasts. He's graceful, kissing, touching, slowly easing himself in and out. I'm lost in the translation of how badly he truly wants me.

"Jules," he gasps.

"Jiles," I correct him despite how tossed around in lust I am.

"Jiles, sorry," he laughs.

Our passion reaches a height I've never known, maybe because there was nothing passionate about the pain of losing your virginity and Cory is the first person I've ever lusted over and wanted. I hope it's more than lust, because I'm so smitten with everything about him. It's weird how I wanted him before I truly knew him as a person, but it turns out I was right about everything. Maybe our instincts just pick up on that shit and that's why my body wanted him more than my brain understood. I run my hand through his terribly soft red strands, feeling the heat and sweat over his neck, some of it even dripping onto me. I'm sure I'm just as moist, reeling in the heat that only his body could make me feel. It's hot in Austin, but it's way hotter in Cory's pants.

As he's pressing himself further into me and we're both panting from this restless activity, I look into his eyes and stare at his oddly long eyelashes. His face is such an odd place to stare at during this love making, not because I'm shy but because I just know that everything he thinks is somehow apparent. If I could see clearly enough I could know in his eyes that he's wanted me for longer than I thought, that his lips are desperate for mine more than I ever might have guessed.

Cory's arms tremble and even shake me as he releases, a gorgeous listening session for me of his final laments at how damn good I felt. I too let out the last of my purrs but am quickly silenced when he decides he needs to caress his tongue with mine.

"Could you really hear me through the walls?" Cory asks as he rolls over to lay on his side facing me. His hand traces my body and rests along my navel.

"Yes, and those ice girls talk so loud I could hear them too."

"Oh geez, I'm sorry. If it makes you feel any better, I overheard you and Kal. Listening to you moan made me hard," he snickers, gazing into my eyes for a good reaction.

"Did you jerk it?"

"Honestly? No, I was too bothered. I couldn't understand why I was so jealous because I'd never looked at you that way before. I googled you that night and read your bio, looked at some photos of you. I started seeing more and more what a cool woman you are and the next time I saw you, I finally saw it all."

"So what's this going to be, are we a couple?" I ask even though I don't think I'm ready to hear the answer.

"I don't know. How about we go on a date and just take it from there?"

"Sounds good dude."

"Why did you call your ex husband a true colours dude bro?"

"It's a joke from the Ben and Brodie show. But I'm sure it went over his head."

"That was lame as hell of him and that girl to show up at your own damn party."

"I was bothered by it but in the end I'd rather be the bigger person. If you don't mind me asking, what happened to Vicki?"

"I broke up with her the day after I tried to sleep with you. She acted like a baby but I'm sure it was just for show, she knows she's got a line of guys waiting for her."

"It seems like every one of those chicks has guys waiting in the wood works for them. They must have golden pussies that pour beer."

"You would think. She was nice, Vicki, but she was too spoiled and needy. I can't understand why any woman would want a life where instead of taking the moose by the antlers, they just want to hop onto some guy and sit on their ass. Do these girls not know the divorce rate? At some point they may be completely broke with nothing."

"I don't think it has ever phased them one bit. Vicki is probably the first girl who has ever been dumped on that squad."

"Didn't your ex dump Katie?"

"He never told me for sure, but I can only assume so otherwise it was mad lame of him to ask me to take him back. Not to mention her hitting on you. Was she really that good looking?" I say, even if I truly don't want to hear his reaction to her rocking body.

"Honestly, I can see why everyone wants her, but not for myself. I guess when I see her, all I can see is how angry I am that she hurt you."

I cannot understand what the appropriate response is to this because of all people to ever say this, the last person I ever expected to say this to me was him. I imagine I'm drooling at the side of my mouth so I pat my skin a few times to ensure that I'm not. Cory doesn't seem to notice all of the silly antics I partake in to make sure I'm not making a complete fool of myself on what I could consider the best night of my life. There's something so unrealistic in this equation; it must be because I'm in it.

"We're going to Ottawa next week, as I can only assume you already know," he interjects while I'm busy analyzing my foolish folly of activity.

"I do," I lie. So maybe I'm not the best about schedules.

"I think you should fly out there and come to the game."

"You're kidding!" Reginald makes his way back into my body form. My floppy frog mouth droops down to the pillow. Ribbit.

"You should take me to your parent's house. I would love to see the look on their faces when they see me. I bet it would be funnier than the look you first gave me," he teases, poking me on the cheek.

"You want to meet MY family?" I say, quickly imaging my entire family a group of tadpoles, all of us in complete shock that a hockey player of our team would be on our property.

"Why not? I see a bright future with you."

"Wowza Cory."

"Is that too much?"

"No, it's just, I thought being a stand up comedian was a high. But the idea of you meeting my family when it felt like my love life was completely hopeless for god knows how many years, I can hardly believe it. It feels like I've won the *Stanley Cup* of life."

"Maybe it's because you have," he kisses me on the chin as I stare at the ceiling with more optimism than I ever felt possible. "By the way, was I better than Kal?"

"We can discuss that later."

There's no way I'm going to spoil this moment by telling Cory that Kal has a bigger....heart!

# CHAPTER 26

You know your life is rad when at least three people at Austin Bergstrom International Airport recognize you. To be fair, two of the people that did had to overlook my photo ID but whatever, it's the name that counts. My name is pretty stand out-ish for a woman so I can see why I stick out like a sore thumb. I wouldn't expect most people to know that I was named after Jiles Perry Richardson AKA *The Big Bopper*, a founding father of rock and roll. My family were even more ecstatic that I married a guy whose last name was Richardson. They felt it was meant to be and I did too. But I think they'd much rather me be with a hockey player than a snotty cunt. Besides, I would never look good in chantilly lace. Truth be told, I have no clue what that is, but if it's sexy, it's not for me.

My flight has a layover in Toronto and even if I'm just at the airport, knowing I'm in my home country warms my heart. I can't recall the last time I saw moose items for sale as a regular trade. I hate to embody a stereotype but moose are a big a part of me as is hockey. No maple syrup though, I hate being sticky. Semen is bad enough!

I wish I could have flown with Cory but the *NHL* are pretty strict about their rules with players. Cory is lucky that there is no game for a few days after his Partisans game. This means he doesn't have to leave immediately with everyone else. He bought his own flight back with me so we intend to share a cozy few days enjoying our favourite town. I haven't told my family yet about Cory, just that I'm coming home for a few days. I bought a copy of my show so we can all enjoy it. The sad part is, I think my family will be more interested in Cory than my show.

When I finally touch down at Ottawa MacDonald Airport, I find my ma and pa waiting for me in their *Ford* station wagon. I don't like that it's a *Ford*, but I did before. The car is so old but my family are the type to get attached to things and not let them go. This explains why I am still playing with moose dolls when I'm 25. I think I'll offer to buy them a new car since I'm such a high roller.

"JILES!" my mother exclaims, leaping out of the car to chase me down as I enter the street. It's the coldest weather I've felt in a long time (my tour being in the summer after all) but I have so much experience under my belt that it doesn't faze me at all.

"Come on ma, it's cold! Get back in the car!" I attempt to shoo her away but she follows me to the back where I place my luggage in the wide trunk.

"I'm just so happy you're here!"

"You saw me a few months ago on my tour ma," I jump in the car as does she in the back seat with me. She really wants to be close. I think about what Brodie told me and decide I am lucky to be in this moment. I hold her hand and tell her and dad all about the rest of my tour, and how my show went too.

Even when I'm talking I keep an eye out on the outside. My dad opts for the scenic route on Queen Elizabeth Drive so I can admire the Rideau Canal. Maybe one day instead of watching the people on the bike, I could be the people on the bike...nah.

**P**ractically everyone in my family comes by as we watch my DVD. It's the first time I've watched it too. I'm pretty shy about the fact that my family are watching me talk about my vagina, having sex with a hockey player (neither of which I've told them about), and other such situations that would never be shared with family in any normal circumstances. Every now and then I see my mother blush and dad looks at her to see if she feels shocked to hear her daughter utter the word "cunt." It's a good thing they already know what type of woman I am. When the DVD is over, my family turns around and stares at me like I was supposed to prepare a speech.

"Well...what did you think?" I ask as I face their waiting eyes. I've got my 'rents, my brother Clarke, two cousins, grandma, and a few aunts and uncles. We managed to fit our smorgasbord of people into the living room.

"Did you really have sex with a hockey player?" Grandma of all people asks me. I stammer for a minute, lip quivering as I debate if I will tell the truth.

"Yeah, I did."

"WHO?" they all start hounding me like *TMZ*.

"Uh, uh...Kal K."

"KARGMAN? OH MY GOD!" my female cousin jumps up. "He is so hot! How did you meet him?!"

"I met him because my neighbor got me into the locker room area at the Trenton."

"How does your neighbor get access to the Assassins

locker room?!" my brother squeals. Like I said, hockey to Canada is exactly what you think it would be. They're losing their shit more than I did when I found Cory Koenig next door. Speaking of which, the door bell rings and I know it's him.

"You'll see," I provide a cheeky smile as I go open the front door. Sure enough, Cory is standing there and looking hotter than ever. It's like he's my prom date, looking all gussied up but it's really just his normal appearance. He's in jeans, a Partisans cap, and a light jacket since he too is immune to the elements.

"You ready?" I whisper. Cory grins and nods his head without speaking since he's just as excited to present himself.

"Everyone, meet my neighbor, and the guy I'm seeing....Cory Ko-"

My cousin cuts me off yet again.

"CORY KOENIG!" she screams and everyone else loses their shit too. They are clearly more proud of me bringing home a former Partisan than me bringing home my DVD.

Cory cannot help but laugh over their great enthusiasm. He stands beside me, going in to hold my hand even. I look up at him and he back at me, both of us with unmatched happiness that our lives are in such good situations. How often do two people get the career of their dreams and find love?

"Cory, as you all know, got traded to Austin and he just happened to move in next door to me. It was a nice surprise to find him there when I came back from my tour."

"Why would you date my sister when you could have any chick in Ottawa?!" my brother chimes in. What a douche.

Cory laughs for a minute before saying some shit that will have my family on their knees.

"A lot of beautiful women flirted me with in Austin, including some familiar faces to Jiles, but I decided I'd rather be with a woman who was more concerned with her own passions than what she looked like to everyone else."

My mom and dad are cheesing harder than anyone else, holding hands themselves and leaning in like a photo is being taken. I know they have absolutely forgotten about Ford, which was also a huge damper on their summer. It feels good to know how much I've surprised everyone with my new life.

"First you put a video of your butt for the world to see on the internet and now you're banging hockey players! My Jiles you really have grown up!" my grandma erupts with apparently no feelings of shame or awkwardness on her sweet, little old lady face. Cory and I are ready to explode with laughter at this off the wall comment.

"Oh, and I got you all seats at the game tonight," Cory changes the topic while kissing their asses, handing me a stack of tickets for the Ottawa Partisans. "I hope you will root for me, but I totally understand if you don't."

Cory is to my family what Oprah is to her audience when she gives away oodles of gifts. My cousins, brother, aunts, uncles, grandma, mom and dad have sure enough all turned into Reginald the frogs, bouncing around the room with more glee than I've ever seen produced at a family reunion. I'm very happy that I am a part of this equation, but more so because Cory is the one that is piecing my life back together.

I take into account how Brodie must feel, almost never getting to experience anything like this. I take a seat at my mom's old desktop while everyone hounds Cory for a photo. He completely obliges, just happy to know that everyone in Ottawa still loves him like he never even left.

I quickly purchase a gift card worth a round trip flight to Melbourne and send Ben a text. I ask him to print this sheet I'm emailing him as well as something I've typed up on a word processor. He's at a remote with Brodie and they are wrapping up for the afternoon.

"Put this in Brodie's gym bag before she leaves for her work out, eh?"

"Sure thing kiddo. How is Canada?"

"Cold, you couldn't handle it. You'll have to come out here some time in the summer. But I doubt my family will be as happy to see you as they are with Cory. Fucking madhouse in here."

"Good for you Jiles, you deserve it. And you owe me a dollar, foreign texts costs .25 each."

Ben prints out the sheets after they pack up the station van and drops them into Brodie's gym bag. When Brodie arrives at cross fit, she sits down in their sleek locker room to change her outfit and finds my gift.

*"Brodie,*

*No one made me realize how good I have it until you pointed it out to me. I hope I can do the same for you. Redeem this sheet for two weeks of substitution on the Ben and Brodie show, free of charge.*

*Love,*
*JP*

*P.S. Look at the sheet below."*

Brodie thumbs to the next page to see an airline gift certificate for $2500. A tear rolls down her cheek before Hitler yells at her to get ready to sweat her ass off.

"Ms. Lane, get your ass going, this isn't the library!"

"Yes ma'am," she hops and skips out, a super smile tattooed on her toned skin. I've given her enough fuel to make this her best work out yet.

I always said I wished I would win an award for my work the way hockey players have a chance to compete, but this feels like so much more than that. Things are on the up and up for my once perpetually drunken ass, I just wish I could say the same for those Austin Ass- I mean the Assassins, my second favourite team. But don't worry, I won't root for them tonight.

I spin the computer chair around and see Cory feeling at home as ever. I lean back in my chair and sigh in relief. Being with my loved ones never felt so good. Better than an orgasm? Of course not but you get my drift!

# CHAPTER 27

The game was a hoot. Initially we thought we wanted to sit in the glam suites but realized how dumb it is to pay more money (not that we paid) to sit further away. After all, we aren't there to socialize. Not one of us wants to talk to each other if we don't have to! We pile in a few rows behind the team bench, just lucky that these tickets were available. Because the Partisans knew Cory would want his friends to be at his homecoming game, they reserved him a good section. That was kind as hell of them considering how much those tickets would have made the team. There's more heart in the organization than you would think.

Austin barely ties it to go into overtime but in the end the Partisans won. I think Cory is secretly happy because he still loves Ottawa and wants to come back. We all give him a standing ovation when he holds his stick up to his former home and salutes his old fan base. We make eye contact and it still boggles my mind that in a sea of fans he is able to spot me so quickly. He really is attracted to me.

Cory also hooked us up with VIP passes so we scoot along down and gather in the hall to see the team after the press badger them for how they felt about his return. Cory comes out quickly and gives me a kiss in front of everyone, which even I wasn't expecting. I figured he would be embarrassed of me.

Slowly but surely the team starts pouring out and they all come talk to Cory, then to me. A few of them know of me for my roots and recent tour. My family goes gaga over them and they all oblige to autographs. We made plans to have drinks with some of the guys post game even, and thankfully most of my family are old and went home. Only my cousins and brother stuck around, and I have this gut feeling my cousin is currently boning a player. Good for her I say, someone besides the ice girls should get a chance at their cocks.

When the night winds down, Cory comes over and sits in my childhood bed Indian style across from me.

"I feel like I'm in a scene from *Sixteen Candles*," I cannot help but point out.

"Make a wish."

"It already came true," I cheesily quip. We both laugh before Cory leans down to kiss me just like the film.

"By the way, I got something for you, I noticed you didn't have this team," Cory says as he reaches into his messenger bag beside my bed. Low and behold....

"You found Albert Louis?!"

"Who?"

"I've been looking for Albert Louis Moose for like 3 years, I kid you not! I cried my eyes out trying to find this little guy. Thank you so much Cory," I began to cry tears of joy even. I cannot believe it. I never thought I'd see Edmonton Moose again.

"I saw him at the Ottawa team store. I thought I'd help finish off your collection."

"You have no idea how much this means to me," I kiss his cheek, clinging dearly to the moose, the one that got away. Looks like everything that got away has come back to me. Moose and self esteem.

"It's so wild to have you in my bedroom. I remember watching so many Partisans games here in high school and winter breaks when I'd come home from *UTA*. I remember the first time I saw you even, it was 2010 and my last winter home before I stayed put in Texas. I thought you were the most impressive rookie I'd seen in a while. And naturally I rubbed one out."

"Well thank you Jiles. I'm sorry I missed my chance to see you here on your tour. I feel like it was a total disrespect to our unknown future, ya know? Like somehow, I cosmically fucked things up. It would have been so much more amazing had you seen me and I completely recognized you too," he laments, resentment overshadowing his face.

"Don't beat yourself up, what matters is that you're here now."

"Should I stay here or go crash with an old teammate for the week?"

"You're kidding right? My family would love to see you come out of my bedroom. It will just confirm what a badass I've become," I laugh, falling back to land on my pillows where I set Albert aside so he can get some zzz's. Cory crawls over and lays down just the same. We sit here and stare up at my ceiling much like the night when he drunkenly crashed.

"Haha, if you say so. What do you want to do? The night is still fairly young in my opinion. 12am and we have nothing to do for days."

"It is a gift and a curse to be so free. I feel like I never use my time wisely."

"I think being with your family is a very wise way to spend it."

"Where is your family?" I ask him, realizing such an integral question I had yet to ponder.

"They still live in my hometown of Dearborn, Michigan, so they come see my games when I pass through. They used to come to Ottawa once in a while, but they don't like coming this much farther north in bad weather," Cory looks over at me. I can tell he is slightly hurt that they were not in attendance on his big night.

"I understand," I put my hand on his and give him a light squeeze. A there there, I'm here kinda touch. "Well, my family is your family. They would always love to have you over."

"I wouldn't expect any less from Ottawa. Man do I miss it here or what?"

"Me too, but sometimes you have to let what you think is right go and find what you think may be even better. All things considered, I made the right choice going to the states. Who would have thought that I needed to get to Texas to meet you?"

"I think maybe deep down we needed a piece of home somewhere so far away from our normal element. This was my first big move and I cannot tell you how much I secretly dreaded it. I mean I left for college but it was hardly far at all, so this felt like my first real time away from home. I basically grew up with the guys I played with on the Manitoba farm team and even some of the Partisans. When I thought about being in Texas where I had not a single acquaintance, I nearly cried. How lucky was I to find you next door? I feel like I shut you out when I first met you, and I'm truly sorry for that."

"Don't be, I was in a bad place, you could see it all over my face."

"How can that be when all I see is beauty and luck?' he compliments me, looking over and letting me fall miles into his sky blue eyes. That may have been the most gorgeous thing anyone has ever said to me. "On the topic of luck, am I getting lucky tonight?" he smirks with a sexy little twist. Ooh boy.

"Getting laid in my childhood bedroom, finally. It will be the first time a cock has ever seen the light of day in here. 16 year old Jiles would be smiling a plenty down at me."

"She'll be giving you way more than a smile in a few minutes."

Cory quickly ambushes my waist and rolls me over on top of him. How macho! He tosses some very in the heat of the moment kisses on me while reaching in under my old Partisans t-shirt with his name on it and the A for his old status as alternate captain. As he's about to remove it, he pulls back.

"Leave the shirt on, it's kind of a turn on," he shyly bites his lip, looking for the passion well within my heart.

"Aye aye, alternate captain," I salute him before

shutting him up with another lip lock.

You don't need me to give you the details of where this night is going, or for the rest of my life with this guy. This is Reginald the Frog signing off from Ottawa, Ontario in Jiles Perry's bedroom, getting laid by Cory Koenig. Hope to catch you next time you're craving some comedic entertainment from a ballsy Canuck sweating her ass off in the Lone Star State. *Woob woob woob, nyuck nyuck nyuck.*

# EPILOGUE

Cory and I stand in the hallway in front of the locker room a few minutes before his game is to begin. It's April Fools day, my favourite day of the year.

"I've got something lined up for tonight," I explain after I kiss him on the cheek. He's in his full gear, even down to his gloves. Damn he's so sexy. Even if some of his equipment smells like sweat and balls.

"You're always full of surprises. I love you babe," he leans down and kisses me.

"I love you too," I murmur, still hideously close to his lips. His warmth on my body is so comforting. I think I love everything there is to love about this man.

"Jiles?"

We both stop and look over. Oh shit. It's Kal Kargman. I forgot they were playing the Vancouver Moose again.

"Uh...hi Kal," I tremble, quickly pushing Cory off of me.

"What's going on? Are you two dating?"

"Um. Sort of," I admit. Cory stays quiet.

"You stole my girl, Cory?" Kal asks him, coming inches from his face. Oh boy, he's pissed.

"Sorry man. I kind of fell in love with her."

"Oh you kind of huh? We will take this out on the ice," he begrudgingly snares before turning around. He storms off in his skates and manages to slam them down without even swaying once in his walk.

"If it makes you feel any better Kal, you've got a bigger dick!" I shout to him.

"WHAT?" Cory eyeballs me with his own anger.

"I said stick, he's got a bigger stick! His is made by *Reebok*, and yours is another brand. God, you never listen to anything I say!" I cover up and walk off quickly, *woob-woobing* on my way out.

𝕯uring the second period, I step out with Canon on the second floor platform where the ice girls do their dances. I'm ashamed to admit I'm wearing their outfit. I don't look too horrible in this get up. That's because they had it custom made with a smaller bust and butt area. For April Fools they are letting me, Austin's biggest hockey lover, do a dance. And I don't even need to tell you it will not be serious dancing. I'm not ashamed to dance because unfortunately they've all seen me dancing with my ass hanging out so this is hardly a comparison.

The whistle blows to start out the period; we're performing during the first break for clean up. I watch in awe as Cory steals the puck over and over from the Moose' first offense line, practically doing all the work as his mates aren't that talented. I also see Kal on the other end of the ice, staying near Baker to protect the net.

The play ends with a save from Baker and it's my time to shine.

"Ladies and Gentleman, Austin's Canadian, Jiles Perry!" the announcer calls over the entire arena. All eyes are on me and I'm not nervous at all. Except maybe to be wearing this outfit. "*Move Your Feet*," by *Junior Senior* begins to play, and I begin to make an ass of myself. I just do some general 80's dance moves as I hear the audience begin to laugh. I see Cory is watching me, and even from this far away I can tell he is smiling.

"Look at Jiles go! She's doing the robot now," the announcer gives a play by play. "And now she's doing the Uma Thurman *Pulp Fiction* dance!"

The period resumes after another few minutes of me goofing around. Sadly enough, that left me totally out of breath. Fuck I'm lazy.

"KOENIG!" Kal shouts to Cory as he chases him down on the ice. Kal reaches out and grabs Cory's jersey from behind. Cory turns around just in time to see Kal swinging at him. Cory falls instantly since Kal is quite bigger. Kal proceeds to jump down and starts swinging at Cory. "You stole my girl! You knew I liked Jiles! You didn't even know who she was!"

"KAL, stop it!" Cory yells back, blocking every punch he can from the very tall, dark, and angry defensemen. In the midst of this fight, a play has continued. An Assassin shoots the puck but misses terribly. In fact, he misses so bad that the puck leaves the rink. It goes up, up and BAM.

I barely spot the black flying object before I feel the world's worst punch in the face. I fall back instantly, now on my back on this hard platform. I taste the warm rush of blood gushing down my nose.

"JILES!" both Kal and Cory turn their attention to me, as does the entire arena.

"Jiles Perry got hit with the puck!" the announcer speaks. Well duh, everyone saw!

A few ushers coming running to me, lifting me up as they give me a towel and sit me in a chair. I sit down and feel the spinning sensations and the dumbstruck numbness. As soon as my body snaps out of its daze, I'm know I'm in for a shit ton of pain.

"Are you okay?" Canon rushes over, getting on her knees to hold my arm.

"I'm fine," I say and notice I whistled a bit. What the hell? Oh no...

I feel around with my tongue and taste blood. I also feel a gap. I look down and see one of my front teeth on the ground. SHIT!

Canon hands me the puck like I'm a baby; giving the baby a toy will help it forget the massive pain lingering around.

Despite my imminent pain I stand up and hold the puck up high, smiling wide to show the blood in my mouth and the very apparent gap. They zoom in on me for the jumbo tron with a goofy grin so I can show off my new hockey player look. I peek down and see Cory and Kal standing up, looking at me with pure sorrow.

They shouldn't feel bad for me: I've got two hot *NHL* players earning penalty minutes over me, I've made friends with my former enemies, I'm a famous stand up comedian, and I have the honour of saying I got hit with a puck and lived to tell about it. I'm most definitely living a Canadian's dream.

# About the Author

**Vanessa Guadiana** is basically the real Jiles Perry.

She's been dreaming of a career on *Saturday Night Live* since she was 14, which is the reason she's moved to NYC multiple times to make these goals come true. Life isn't always that kind, and now she is a CDL driver trucking across the US and Canada, getting weird looks and being confused for a hooker or a drug mule everywhere she goes. She currently resides nowhere and has no kids because they are annoying.

Vanessa is from Detroit but was raised in Dallas, where she earned her bachelor's in creative writing at the University of Texas at Dallas. She also has numerous comedy classes under her belt from *UCB Theatre*, *The Pit*, and *Dallas Comedy House*. Vanessa performs stand up comedy and blogs about hockey and hot gingers at:

## VanessaLovesHockey.com

Made in the USA
Coppell, TX
24 December 2020